GOULART PAPRIKASH

Here is another of Ron Goulart's futurological epics that answers such universally important questions as:

Do catmen eat mice?

Is the king of Laranja East also its phantom killer?

Is the heir to the Starbuck billions an impostor?

Can a beautiful highwayperson find love and happiness in the clink?

Can a robot judge dispense impartial justice if his eye-lens has been poked out?

How does one get dinner after the robot chef has blown up?

Do catmen eat mice?

Once again the perceptive and deeply concerned mind of the non-Hugo-winning author of THE TIN ANGEL, SPACE-HAWK INC., WHEN THE WAKER SLEEPS, and FLUX has produced a novel of the Barnum System guaranteed to . . .

Ron Goulart

A WHIFF OF MADNESS

DAW BOOKS, INC.
DONALD A. WOLLHEIM, PUBLISHER

1301 Avenue of the Americas
New York, N. Y.   10019

Published by
THE NEW AMERICAN LIBRARY
OF CANADA LIMITED

First Printing, August 1976

1 2 3 4 5 6 7 8 9

PRINTED IN CANADA
COVER PRINTED IN U.S.A.

CHAPTER 1

The lizardman, lycra cloak fluttering and allseason turban jiggling, came charging across the vast chill lobby of the publishing center. He planted himself directly in the path of Jack Summer. "A fine hour to be arriving for work!" he boomed. "Where is she?"

"Who?" Summer was a middle-sized, wiry, sandy-haired man of thirty-one, and right now his skin was tanned that particular shade you get after a few weeks on Neptune. He glanced up at one of the several ballclocks that floated here and there in the Coultdrome lobby. "Eleven A.M. Barnum Standard Time isn't—"

"My wife, that's who!" The large greenish lizardman gave his turban an angry adjusting pat. "My wife! She ran off with you! Which is—"

"Wait now," Summer told him. "I admit I've run off with a girl on occasion, but never with a lizard."

The lizardman gave an openmouthed snort, causing his forked tongue to unfurl and snap. "Not one of my lizard wives, you pink-cheeked gigolo!" After another snort he tugged a fat wallet out of one of his cloak pockets. A flick of his green scaly wrist snapped the wallet open, allowing a string of glossy tri-op photos to unfold. "One of my humanoid wives!"

" . . . Sixteen, seventeen," counted Summer. "Quite a collection."

"This is the one to which, as if you didn't know, I allude!" A green finger jabbed the thirteenth photo from the top. "This one! Her name is Lorna!"

"Lorna." Summer leaned down to study the picture of the ravishing, sparsely clothed blond. "Name doesn't ring a bell, and I can't say I've ever—"

"Doesn't ring a bell!" bellowed the lizardman, tugging at something else under his cloak. "My second most favorite humanoid wife departs from my happy home, leaving nothing behind save a scribbled note indicating she's fled with you, and you babble about bells ringing!" He yanked a horsewhip free. "I vowed I'd horsewhip any man who dared—"

"Is that what that is you're clutching, a horsewhip?"

"Yes, and you little realize the trouble I had procuring this one! Since there are no horses here on Barnum, I had to have this one teleported all the way from—"

"Lorna, did you say?" Summer reached into a pocket of his tunic. "It's possible I do remember her after all. Let me consult my addresswheel and perhaps . . ." A stungun appeared in Summer's tan hand. He fired directly at the outraged husband.

The lizardman froze, horsewhip half raised.

Summer put his gun away, gestured at two guards across the publishing building lobby. "Dump this guy someplace," he suggested.

The catman guard said, "Golly, Summer, you roving reporters surely lead a roguish life."

The other, a chubby human, asked, "Did you really run off with this gent's wife?"

"No, but I think maybe she's the blond who grabbed my private parts during the masked ball on the spaceliner trip back from Neptune," answered the reporter. "Lord knows who she really ran off with."

"Ah, the muckraking life." The catman sighed while taking hold of the stunned lizard by the elbow. "Standing guard for Mr. Coult you never get your private parts gr—"

"Should a ravishing blond, with her hair over one eye like this, show up in quest of me tell her I've been sent to some planet like Murdstone to do a *Muckrake* Magazine story."

"Sure thing, Summer," said the chubby guard. "Would you mind if I made a play for—"

"Nope, that would be an excellent idea." He left them, then hurried across to an ascend tube.

A naked black girl was standing next to the entrance door. "Welcome back, Jack."

"Hi, Nardis." The door whooshed open and he allowed her to enter the chute ahead of him.

"I hope this thing lets me out on the right floor this time," said Nardis. "I'm due up at *Galactic Knitting* to pose for a cover."

The powerful currents of air wafted them upward. "I didn't know you could knit."

She scratched a buttock. "Oh, yes, I have terrible domestic urges sometimes. Last night I baked a pie. I suppose I ought to get help."

"Or move to another planet. Now on Neptune, in the Earth System, they still—"

"I read the pieces you did from Neptune, Jack, on that water rights scandal. Very incisive."

A door opened and Summer was tossed out of the

chute before he could reply. Joyous pipe-organ music surrounded him on his way to the *Muckrake* editorial-floor reception desk. "Hello, Pepper."

The lovely green girl kneeling behind the darkwood desk said, "Oh, howdy, Jack. Excuse me if I don't give you a welcome-back hug."

Summer was studying the stained glass windows and the icons, sniffing at the incense smell in the air. "Coult changed the decor again."

"His wife did."

"I thought she favored Old West Earth."

"Different wife," replied Pepper. "Mr. Flowers is in the conference room down at the end of Corridor C. Oh, and don't forget to genuflect before you go in."

"I'll try. Bye, Pepper."

"Thought your pieces on the Neptune water business were very incisive, Jack."

"Thanks."

The organ music followed him down the somber corridors and into the large Gothic cathedral which was apparently the new editorial conference room. "Fred?"

"Up here, Jack." His weary, lanky editor was seated in a pew toward the front of the church, near a life-size statue of a four-armed blue saint. "Here under Blessed Mother Malley."

Overcoming an impulse to tiptoe, the reporter strode down to sit next to Fred Flowers. "This wife's taste isn't quite up to the last one."

"She's an even larger bimbo, too," said his tired-looking editor. "Well, let's see if I can give you your new assignment before the choirboys get back."

"Choirboys?"

"We get 'em every hour on the hour; supposed to be uplifting. A hundred of the little buggers, made by a Swiss watchmaker on Murdstone, and every damn one of 'em is towheaded and freckled." Flowers jabbed at his gaunt cheeks to indicate where some of the freckles appeared. "I want you to go out to Peregrine, Jack."

"That looks like Coult himself in that stained glass window there," observed Summer, pointing with a thumb, "sitting at the right hand of God."

"It is; the bimbo with the halo is the current wife of the enormous Coult publishing empire."

"Don't much like women with their hair down over one eye like that."

"She has a very interesting backside, so I'm told," said Flowers. "Now about this assignment on the planet Peregrine."

"Yeah, she does have a nice ass, now you mention it. Something you don't often see in stained glass window figures." Summer returned his attention to his editor. "What do you want me to write about on Peregrine, the civil war?"

"Everybody knows civil wars are corrupt. *Muckrake*'s readers are tired of that sort of exposé," said the weary Flowers, slumping farther down in his pew. "What I want you to dig into for me is a little scandal concerning King Waldo the second."

"He's the ruler of Laranja East, isn't he? Laranja East and Laranja West are the territories having the civil war."

"Yep," replied Flowers. "Our stringer out there sent us word King Waldo is killing people."

"Is that newsworthy? Kings and presidents are always—"

"This guy is putting on a slouch hat, a black cloak, and gray gloves, Jack, to strangle little old ladies. Our stringer—"

"You mean King Waldo is the Phantom of the Fog?"

"Looks very possible. Seems he—"

Bong!

The cathedral vibrated as an unseen bell tower struck the half hour.

"Oh, that nitwit bimbo and her interesting backside." Flowers grimaced. "Anyway, Jack, there appears to be a strong likelihood the good king is the phantom strangler. Lots of rumors to that effect are floating around the territory."

"Has the palace had anything to say about the charges?"

"The king's press secretary maintains it's a media plot to smear the monarch."

Summer toyed with the prayerwheel dangling from a hook on the back of the pew in front of him. "Whether or not Waldo's the killer, he's not going to take kindly to my walking into his territory to nose around."

"Yep, the king's very touchy about the rumors that he's a crazed pattern murderer. At his last press conference he threatened to horsewhip the newsman who—"

"That's right, they have horses out there," said Summer. "Okay, so I'm going to need a cover story, a plausible reason for being there."

From a wrinkled pocket in his rumpled tunic the

editor withdrew a photo of a plump, shaggy-feathered birdman. Holding the photo out to Summer, he said, "This lad claims to be Mulligan Starbuck."

"So?"

"Mulligan was lost at sea at the tender age of nine, twenty-two long years ago." Flowers dropped the picture on Summer's lap. "Five weeks ago, according to our Peregrine stringer, this fellow in the photo appeared on the doorstep of the Starbuck estate in the Laranja East countryside. He swears he's the missing Mulligan, the long-lost heir come home to roost."

"I've heard of the Starbucks. Lot of money."

"Right, the Starbucks are one of the richest families on the planet. They're in railroads, oil, steel, copper, and weapons. With the war between East and West in full swing, they're raking in fantastic profits."

"The head of the family is Wattas Starbuck, as I recall. What's he think about this claimant?"

"Denies entirely he's little Mulligan grown to manhood. However, Wattas's old mother, Lady Thorkin, has accepted the lad. She believes in her heart he's her long missing grandson and h s given him the run of the estate, making for some tension around the Starbuck homestead. The Starbuck claimant affair is causing quite a frumus, charges of fraud are in the air, and there may well be a trial." Flowers slumped a bit more. "It's the kind of situation *Muckrake* might well write up."

"I should be able to convince Waldo's people, and anyone else curious, I'm in Laranja to dig into the Starbuck affair."

Flowers closed his eyes for a few seconds. The light from one of the stained glass windows made rainbow patterns across his weary, lined face. "Something else I better tell you, Jack. We're going to need pictures and I have to assign you, somewhat against my will, a partner. If you can get me a shot of King Waldo skulking through the foggy back streets of the capital city in his phantom gear, or maybe actually in the act of grabbing some old bimbo by the throat I'll—"

"Palma!" realized Summer. "You're teaming me up again with Palma, the horniest photographer in the Barnum System . . . if not the entire cosmos."

"Yep, him," admitted the editor. "He claims he's reformed, after getting himself almost killed on Malagra."

"Malagra, the pesthole of the universe. Is Palma still there?"

"No, he's on Peregrine, doing a picturespread on the public executions in Laranja East," said the weary Flowers. "Therefore, he's got a perfectly respectable excuse for being in the territory."

"I doubt Palma's much reformed," said Summer. "Every time we've worked together in the past he—"

"Glorious! Glorious! Glorious!"

Little automaton choirboys were marching out onto the cathedral altar, singing.

"You're ten minutes ahead of schedule, you little clockwork twerps!" Flowers shouted at them.

"Glorious! Glorious! Glorious!"

Standing, Summer said, "I'll pack. When do I depart for Peregrine?"

"Ten tomorrow from Barnum Spaceport-two," said his editor. "Try to keep Palma from causing an incident, will you? Don't go screwing around too much yourself."

"I assure you," said Summer, grinning, "Palma's behavior and mine will be nothing less than saintly."

Flowers sighed. "Well, good luck."

"Glorious! Glorious! Glorious!" sang the choirboys.

CHAPTER 2

The parade flowed along the wide cobblestone street. A marching band of scarlet-uniformed birdmen passed the corner where Summer had been forced to stop because of the thick crowd of parade watchers. It was forty degrees Celsius on the glaring midday streets of the capital city of Laranja East. The newly arrived reporter was anxious to get to the Laranja-Sheraton and out of the sun.

"Excuse me," he said to the twin fat ladies immediately in front of him.

They continued licking at their strawberry ice cream cones, ignoring him.

Six dozen steam-operated military robots went clanking by, followed by several squads of virginal young blond girls in white lycra tunics. Each girl carried a placard that said: KILL THE DIRTY BASTARD!

Summer managed to nudge a few paces to the left, which brought him up against a broad, feathered back. "Mind if I try to cross?"

The birdman kept pecking at his suetburger, moving not.

Virginal redheads trooped by. CUT HIM IN CHUNKS! SPILL HIS GUTS!

"Pardon me." Summer elbowed around the hefty

14

birdman, shoved one of the fat ladies aside, and made it to the edge of the curbstone.

A dozen gold-braided policemen were galloping by, mounted on white stallions.

"My, look at those horsewhips, so many of them," remarked a fat lady.

"What do you suppose the man without his pants is meant to represent?" asked her twin.

"What man without pants, Alma?"

"Right there, Dolores, that bald man trotting along in the wake of the horsemen with the dozen or more angry high priests in hot pursuit."

"Palma!" said Summer.

It was indeed the bald photographer, clad in a candy-striped singlet and a pair of sky-blue briefs. The howling catmen on his trail wore flowing black and gold robes, and were waving double-edged golden swords. "Sacrilege! Defilement!" they were shouting. "Profanation!"

Dodging white horses, Summer reached his friend's side to begin running with him. "You were supposed to refrain from trouble."

"I'm trying," panted Palma, "I'm trying. That's why I'm attempting to outrun this particular bunch of crazed fanatics."

"Sacrilege! Debasement!" cried the nearest robed catmen, who were not more than a dozen feet behind.

"What did you debase?"

"Oh," said Palma, "I merely patted a nun on the keaster."

Sprinting, Summer got alongside one of the galloping policemen. "You won't mind my borrowing this?" He tugged the horsewhip out of its saddle holster.

Stopping where he stood, Summer told Palma, "Head for that alley over there." He cracked the whip, tufts of fur fluttered up in the glaring air, and the lead priest fell down. While the whip was still wound around the fallen man's furry ankle, Summer jerked it and caused the priest to trip the next two pursuers.

Palma meanwhile was streaking for the narrow alley between two towering neobrick buildings.

After felling three more priests and avoiding the angered mounted policeman, Summer took off. In the alley he asked, "Why'd you stroke some nun on the rear end, anyway?"

Palma sprang for the top of the nearwood fence at the alley's end. "Foolish damn thing to do, since I'm basically a tit man," he admitted. Wheezing, he struggled over the fence and dropped down into the miniature golf course on the other side. "Of course I didn't even realize she was in holy orders, seeing as how she was naked at—"

"How'd she happen to be naked?" Summer joined him on the turf.

Running down the sloping field of the tiny golf course, the bald photographer replied, "Women usually are naked in the ladies' wing of a Turkish bath. See, through a perfectly honest mistake I happened to wander into—"

"Never mind." Summer glanced back over his shoulder. "They've ceased chasing us."

Palma slowed down, wiping his hand across the top of his glistening bald head. He was roughly the same height as Summer, nearly two years older. "You wouldn't expect Quakers to be so vindictive," he said. "Though it may be the Peregrinian splinter—"

"What was the parade about?"

"Nothing much; another public execution this afternoon."

"Fore, for mercy's sake!" cried a dwarf they were approaching. "Fore!" He swung his golf club in the air several times.

"Excuse us." Palma bowed toward the man and his midget spouse. He and Summer had to cross a stone bridge over a small scummy lagoon to reach the street. "Did you happen to notice the knockers on that midget broad? If you multiply those tits by three it's fairly astound—"

"Why are the citizens of Laranja East having a big parade for this public execution?"

"They always have parades, sometimes a carnival or a masked ball," explained Palma. "The girl who ran the bear-baiting concession at the last carnival had a momentous set of chabobs, Jack. The nipples, mind you, measured full—"

"Did you leave your pants at the Turkish bath?"

Palma looked at his unclad lower limbs. He went over and sat on a green lucite street bench. He rubbed at his bald head, not meeting Summer's eyes. "Well, Jack, as a matter of fact, my trousers are at the Galactic Express Teleport station on King Waldo Skyway."

"Oh, so?"

"I went in there to teleport a basket of assorted fruit to a young lady on Malagra in commemoration of her twenty-first birthday," said Palma, "and this brunette who was manning the fruit desk turned out to have the most incredible set of whammos these old orbs have—"

"OK, it'll be easier to buy you a new pair of pants."

"Don't you want to hear the stirring account of how I got from the G.E.T. office to the Turkish—"

"Nope." Summer rested one foot on the bench. "I want to hear about our assignment here."

"Coming along smoothly. We've got an appointment to call at Fallen Oaks tomorrow morning."

"What is Fallen Oaks?"

"The Starbuck estate, some fifty miles to the north of this fair city. We're going to interview and photograph Mulligan Starbuck and his doting granny."

"What about our stringer? I want to talk to him."

"Yeah, he's the editor of the local paper out there, which is entitled the *Starbuck Company Town Weekly*. Only a few miles from the estate; we're to see him after we call on the claimant."

Summer said, "Have you heard anything more about the Phantom of the Fog?"

"He did in another old lady last night," said Palma. "Rumor has it King Waldo the second can't account for his time during the hours when the deed was done."

"Is King Waldo actually the phantom? For that matter, is the claimant really Mulligan Starbuck?" said Summer. "We've got some interesting questions to answer."

"I think better with my pants on," said Palma. "Let's wend our way, unobtrusively, to the nearest fashionable clothier."

CHAPTER 3

———◆———

"A veritable fairyland, eh?" said the owlman who was sharing their first-class railroad carriage with them. He rubbed his gloved hands together while making a satisfied hooting sound. "The lofty towers shimmering in the glowing miasma, the pillars of fire shining like beacons for the weary traveler, eh?"

Palma coughed. "Hard to see the fairyland through all this smoke."

The chuffing steam train was carrying them through mile after mile of factories. Hunching, soot-smeared buildings were set in a forest of spewing smokestacks and chimneys. Columns of orange flame ripped up through the gray smoky morning, millions of sparks flickered, yellowish fog swirled around everything.

"Smoke, sir?" the owlman's eyes went wide; his feathers bristled. "Why, that's the stuff from which dreams are made. That, gentlemen, is the future taking shape under our very noses." From his flowered waistcoat he took a business card. "I don't believe we've introduced ourselves."

"That's true," agreed Summer.

"I am Benton Fruit-Smith."

19

Palma accepted the proffered card. "Work for the Starbucks, eh?"

"Damned proud to be able to answer in the affirmative," said Fruit-Smith. "I'm with the Child Labor Division, a position which allows me ample opportunity to exercise my humanitarian tendencies."

"Like kids, do you?" Palma rolled the business card around his forefinger, tapped it against the sooty window.

"Dote on them, sir," replied Fruit-Smith. "It is one of the sorrows of my life, I must admit, that Mrs. Fruit-Smith and myself have never been blessed with an egg." He rubbed a gloved knuckle at the corner of his eye. "I suppose that's why I'm so concerned with the welfare of the tots and tykes who labor for us in the myriad clean and homelike Starbuck factories. 'You're positively softhearted when it comes to them whelps, Ben,' the foreman of the tallow plant remarked to me only last week. 'Yes, I suppose I am,' was my rejoinder. It breaks my heart whenever one of the little darlings takes a header into a tallow vat. One of my greatest days was the day I persuaded the Starbucks to approve the purchase of a long pole with a hook on the end of it." He blinked at Summer and Palma. "To fish the little rascals out with, do you see?"

Palma sneezed. "You're a very good person, Mr. Fruit-Smith," he said. "In fact, you may well be the very type of person I'm seeking." He paused to stroke one of the cameras hanging around his neck. "I'm always on the lookout for great humanitarians to photograph for *Great Humanitarians* Magazine."

"Ah, sir, I don't feel I'm a great man." The owlman ruffled his chin feathers. "Is it the *Great Humanitari-*

ans assignment which brings you to our territory?"

Palma leaned across the carriage, lowering his voice. "Actually, Mr. Fruit-Smith, and I ask you to keep this confidential—"

"You can count on my discretion, sir."

"My partner and I are here to look into the Starbuck claimant affair."

"Eh?" Fruit-Smith's facial feathers perked up. "Oh, that's a shocking business, sir; a most unfortunate event in the annals of a great family."

"You don't think the claimant is authentic?" asked Summer.

"Not a bit of it, sir." The owlman shook his head. "Why, I once dandled little Mulligan on my knee at a Starbuck Upper Echelon Employees and Their Immediate Families Picnic. I can tell you this great lout is no more Mulligan Starbuck than I am. Indeed he—"

"*Starbuck Company Town Station.*"

"Excuse us, Mr. Fruit-Smith," said the bald photographer. "We must disembark here."

When they were on the platform in front of the shingled station Summer said, "Fruit-Smith should spread our cover story fairly far and wide."

"Let us hope," said Palma. "You know, Jack, I'm getting interested in this Starbuck claimant thing. You think this guy could really—"

"Our main reason for being here is to talk to the editor of the *Starbuck Company Town Weekly*."

"Say, have you noticed the yonkers on that young lady standing over there holding the horsewhip? Observe how they point directly at you. That's what I call an honest tit, one which can look you square in the eye."

The lovely auburn-haired girl approached them now. "Would you be Mr. Summer and Mr. Palma?" she inquired.

"We would," Summer said.

"I'm McNulty, sent from the main house to drive you to your interview with Lady Thorkin and Mr. Mulligan," said the girl.

"Why not allow me to drive," suggested Palma. "It would—"

"Exactly as I surmised." McNulty frowned at him. "You're just exactly the sort who'd like to see me returned to some secondary, subsidiary position ... after I've struggled long and hard to achieve the situation I now have within the Starbuck household. I'll drive the carriage; it's my job."

The carriage was drawn by a pair of brandy-colored horses. Summer climbed in.

Palma hesitated beside the vehicle. "Wouldn't it be more egalitarian if I rode up in front there beside you, Miss McNulty?"

"Suit yourself," replied the girl. "You must promise, though, to make no further comments about my breasts."

Palma bounded up next to her on the driver's seat. "What gave you the idea I was doing that?"

"The simpering expression on your silly face, the moony glint in your eyes." She cracked the whip across the horses' flanks. "Get up there. . . . An interest in breasts is most childish."

"On the contrary." The carriage commenced rolling down a graveled road away from the train station. "My fascination has increased with maturity. When I was a beardless, though curly-haired, lad I had little interest in breasts, as you call them, at all."

"A man of your obvious intelligence should be able to look beyond breasts to the mind within. An intellect has no breasts or secondary sex characteristics."

"I'd hate to think such a thing. For instance . . ."

There were no more factories now, hardly any smoke in the late morning sky. Fields of grass and stands of sturdy trees spread away from both sides of the gently climbing road.

Summer clasped his hands behind his head, and whistled softly with the tip of his tongue pressed to the roof of his mouth.

"How do you do," said the plump birdman who was leaning against the sundial in the north corner of the immense formal garden. "I'm Mulligan Starbuck."

"Like bloody hell," muttered the lizard butler who'd escorted Summer and Palma out here.

"That will be quite enough, Delap."

"Ruddy perishing fraud, says I," said the lizard butler as he departed.

"The servants, alas, haven't all accepted me the way dear Gran has." He gestured with a feathered hand at a white-painted wrought-iron bench. "Won't you please sit down, gentlemen."

Palma did.

Summer remained under a decorative arbor arch. "Does all of the staff—"

"Sit down, hurry up." Mulligan glanced anxiously about. "We don't have much time before the old lady shows up. I have to talk to you."

"About what?" Summer moved nearer.

"Mully? Mully, little pet, where are you?" There was a rattling off in the bamboo sector of the garden. "Mully, don't tease your poor gran."

Mulligan said to Summer, "I want you to know why I'm really—"

"Mully, I fear I'll perish amidst this dreadful bamboo."

"We're right over here by the sundial, dear Gran," called Mulligan. He hit the side of his leg with a fist.

After some more rattling, and a bit of crackling, a very old birdwoman came stumbling into view. She wore a loose-hanging flowered lycra dress, and supported herself with two ebony canes. Her yellow beak was laced with fine cracks; most of the feathers from the top of her head had fallen out. "There he is. There's my sweetest little Mully, my long-lost honeybunch, my little dumpling come back to me from the womb of the vast deep. And good morning to you, gentlemen."

Palma popped to his feet. "Good morning, Lady Thorkin." He bowed over her half-feathered old hand. "I am Palma, the noted photographer, and my associate is the justly famed Jack Summer."

"We're honored that two such esteemed journalists as yourselves," said Lady Thorkin, "have journeyed across the limitless gulf of space to help spread the truth about my little buttercup to the far corners of the universe."

"That's our specialty," Palma told her. "Last year alone we publicized three dumplings, two buttercups—"

Summer cut in. "We'd like to hear what you have to say, Lady Thorkin."

The birdwoman chuckled. "I never tire of discussing my little prodigal dumpling; do I, honeybunch?"

"No, certainly not, Gran." Standing behind her back, Mulligan pointed to himself and then to Summer, silently beaking the words, "Want to talk to you alone."

While guiding the old woman to a wrought-iron chair, Summer shot the claimant a puzzled look. "Why?" he asked out of the corner of his mouth.

"It's about—"

"Hounds!" said Palma.

Barking and baying had started off beyond the rose bushes.

"I'm afraid," said Mulligan, "that Father has let the killer dogs loose again."

CHAPTER 4

"Thank you so much; we'll be relatively safe up here," gasped Lady Thorkin as Palma boosted her to the top of the enormous greenhouse. "You're a real honeybunch, even though you don't have any hair."

The bald photographer took a position near the ancient birdwoman. "Don't have any feathers either, but despite such handicaps—"

"Your father knows we're out here interviewing you, doesn't he?" Summer asked the claimant.

Mulligan was squatting on several neoglass panels. "Oh, yes—which is why he unchained the dogs," he said. "He doesn't approve of my talking to reporters."

Three ferocious Venusian police dogs had located them, and were leaping and snarling directly below.

"Does he approve of the hounds rending your sweet old granny asunder?" inquired Palma.

"He usually calls them off before they do any serious harm. Although last week a caricaturist from *Interstellar Punch* had his—"

Boom! Bam! Boom!

"Goodness me," exclaimed Lady Thorkin, "the steam hounds must be on the blink again."

Chunks of metal began clattering down around them, smashing holes in the neoglass squares.

26

"My father was recently persuaded to add steam-operated robot hounds to his kennel," explained Mulligan. "They don't function as smoothly as he was led to believe; notably the boilers in some of the creatures."

Boom!

"I fear that was Rex," said the old birdwoman.

A plastic dog snout clinked down on Palma's head, bounced off and fell into the greenhouse. "Your favorite robot, was he?"

"Yes, he had a really agreeable personality, for a machine. Many's the time—"

"Are you scoundrels ready to come to terms?" Five more huge and nasty dogs, three real and two steam-driven, had come charging through the shrubs. Close on their heels stalked a middle-aged birdman in a tweed suit.

"It's Father." Mulligan brought his beak close to Summer's ear and lowered his voice. "I won't be able to tell you what I want to now. You'll have to try to get back some—"

"You there, the chap with the hairless pate, are you John Summer?" Wattas Starbuck, surrounded by howling dogs, was shaking a feathery fist at them.

Palma inched closer to the edge of the slightly slanting neoglass roof. "Do you mean to say you don't recognize me? A man whose incisive photographs are known far and wide throughout the Barnum System of planets as well as the Earth System? A photographer whose name is a household word in the farthest reaches of the galaxy. I am Palma."

"If you're not this rogue Summer, I'll thank you to intrude no farther, sir."

"I'm Summer," said Summer.

"Yes, I should have guessed from that sneaky look in your eyes, the mean slant of the mouth, the cringing attitude as you crouch there in abject fear. Obviously you're a journalist."

"We'll have to get together again sometime when you don't have your dogs."

"I doubt not I can best you in a fair combat, sir." He silenced his dogs, who sat staring anxiously at the group atop the greenhouse. "Many a poacher has reason to dread the name of Wattas Starbuck. With naught but these two fists I've—"

"I'm not in the mood to play mine's-bigger-than-yours," cut in Summer. "Do you have anything else you want to chat about?"

"I didn't expect anyone in your profession to be so forthright," said Wattas. "Very well, sir, we will come to the point. This so-called interview was arranged without my knowledge or consent. The Starbuck clan has been enough smeared and maligned by the media. Like our dedicated king, and other great men of the age, we are targets for the unjustified darts of the pygmies of the press. I will allow you and your associate to depart unmolested by myself or my faithful pack of fearsome dogs. You must, however, promise to print not a word about your visit here today. You must, furthermore, never attempt to interview this fawning impostor or my barmy old mum again."

"Oh, Watty, you're not being the dumpling you once—"

"Well, Summer, do I have your word, for what it's worth?"

"Sure," said Summer.

"Hold on, Jack," said Palma. "Freedom of the press is like a flaming sword and we oughtn't to allow our right to speak out to be trampled by a pack of hounds and—"

"Might as well admit we've been beaten," said Summer. "Mr. Starbuck, we accept your terms."

"Good, I assumed you, being a mealymouthed coward at heart, would." Wattas bent close to one of the dogs. "Back to the kennels, the lot of you."

With regretful gazes at their lost prey, the dogs sulked away along the lanes of flowering plants.

"Don't forget," whispered Mulligan just before Summer and Palma leaped to the ground.

When they were passing, with several burly servants close behind, through the outer gates of the Starbuck estate Palma said, "My strong extrasensory powers tell me Wattas Starbuck knew we were coming. He staged his little dog show to impress us."

"No doubt," said Summer. "Let's hope we impressed him with the fact we came to Peregrine solely to interview his spurious son."

The bald photographer was scanning the roadway. "Looks like Miss McNulty and her famous straightforward hangers are not here to give us a lift back to town," he said.

"We'll walk."

"Mulligan conveyed the idea he had something important to tell us." Palma kicked at the white gravel.

"Wants to persuade me he's the real thing."

"Might be more than that," said Palma, stroking his head. "Well, let's see what Mayhew has to say."

"Mayhew?"

"The editor of the weekly."

"I forgot his name."

"Not like you."

Summer halted, stood for nearly a minute staring back at the Starbuck mansion. "Something ..." he said.

"What?"

"I don't know yet."

The lane ran out of cobblestones and turned to dirt. It was midafternoon, but the sky over the company town had a sooty twilight look. The lane was empty except for a dead dog sprawled in front of a narrow tight-shut tailor shop.

"You can't beat a big city for excitement," observed Palma, wiping dust off his scalp.

Spotting the faded *Town Weekly* sign, Summer said, "This street's too empty, too many blinds pulled down, too many shutters up."

"Could be business hereabouts is going through a periodic decline."

Summer approached the neoglass door of the newspaper office slowly. The door stood a few inches open. He pushed it, then went inside the shadowy room beyond.

There was a thick smell of printer's ink in the air, and something else.

"Gunpowder," said Palma.

"They still use that kind of gun on Peregrine." Summer ran for the door marked *Editor*. "Mayhew!"

Something fell down on the other side of the door and wood and papers clattered down.

A small gray-haired man was lying on his side next

to the rolltop desk. His in-box, contents spilled, was on the hardwood floor beside him. There was blood all over him, streaked across the front of his blue shirt, smeared over his arms, still oozing from the three bullet holes in his chest.

Palma reached him first and eased an arm around his shoulders. "Jesus, Mayhew, what—"

"Listen," said the dying editor in a dim, faraway voice, "I found ... found out too much ... they ... didn't like ... two people ... two people you ... must see ... Ferrier ... Dr. Ferrier ... Tully Keep ... try ..." He stopped talking all at once.

Palma lowered Mayhew to the floor, then stood up and away from him. "Dead and gone, the poor bastard. One minute he's sitting here getting out this pathetic little newspaper and then—"

"Let's go," said Summer.

CHAPTER 5

The waiter kept his furry thumb in Summer's soup while journeying across the dim, crowded restaurant from the kitchen to the table. "Here you go, skinhead." He banged the bowl down in front of Palma.

Wiping sloshed soup from his front, the bald photographer said, "You're slightly off target. My friend ordered the stockpot soup, whereas I ordered the garden fresh tossed salad."

The catman shrugged, said, "So pass it across to him," and headed once again for the kitchen.

Palma handed the bowl of thick, greenish soup over to the other side of the small table. "I'm trying to keep my thumb exactly where his was so as not to spread—"

"Why is it," asked Summer, ignoring the bowl of soup, "that on every damn planet in the known universe you unfailingly drag me to the most ungodly eating places ever—"

"Churl's is the most popular restaurant in the capital, Jack. People fight for reservations. I had to bribe three—"

"Catch, Baldy."

A plate of salad came sailing through the smoke-clogged air from a distance of several feet away.

Palma made a valiant grab, but missed.

The plate, shedding folliage, continued on until it smacked a prosperous lizard banker over one ear.

"Lousy catch," remarked their waiter. "I hope you do better on the main course."

Palma rubbed at the salad dressing which had spilled over his scalp when the salad went by. "With a place as popular as Churl's people don't expect to be treated as humans ... or lizards or whatever the case may be."

Summer asked, "What have you found out about the two names Mayhew gave us?"

Licking his fingers, Palma said, "This is vinegar dressing and I ordered thousand island. You'd think—"

"What about those names?"

"OK," said Palma. "First Dr. Ferrier. He's a middle-aged catman, one of the leading biochemists on Peregrine. Teaches right here in Laranja East, at King Waldo University."

"Hey, I forgot your garlic bread." Their waiter, at the kitchen door, tossed half a loaf, sliced, toward their table.

Palma caught three out of the five slices. "Did better with this than with the salad."

The other two slices had bonked the lizard banker on the sconce. He shoved back in his chair, waving a green fist. "I've had, I'll have you know, more than enough of this disgraceful behavior. I happen to be Edgar Allan Boop, and I demand to see the manager at once."

"Garlic bread?" asked Palma.

"No, thanks," said Summer. "What's Ferrier's specialty? Is he tied in with the War Office, helping the government in some way?"

"Far as I can discover, nope. He's simply a highly thought-of professor."

"And Tully Keep?"

Palma said, "He's even more remotely connected with King Waldo and the phantom strangler. Keep heads up a band of guerrillas over near the East-West border someplace."

"Hot plate, hot plate! Watch out!" The catman waiter was dashing around the close-packed tables with a steaming dish held at arm's length. "Yike!" He dropped it a half yard short of their table.

"I was betting you'd make it." Palma studied his spattered boots. "Was that the Grout Stew Churl or my friend's Soyloaf Scallopini?"

"Search me," said the catman. "We got one of them new robot chefs, you know, kind runs on steam. Makes the kitchen hotter to work in than a Turkish bath. On top of that he gets the orders all mixed up." The waiter took a few careful steps back. "Try not to step in any of that till I get a busboy to mop it up."

After running a plyonap over his boots, Palma said, "It may be Mayhew was incoherent by the time we got to him, Jack. The names may not have anything to do with the phantom."

"Even so, we'll check them both out," decided Summer. "Any preferences?"

"Yeah, you'd best take Dr. Ferrier. I have a feeling some of those religious zealots are still skulking around the capital here in search of me or a portion thereof," said Palma. "I'll feel safer out on the road, communing with the wilderness. You encounter a more interesting brand of people the farther you go from the urban milieu. I recall once at an oasis on Jupiter I met a lady anthropologist with a truly over-whelming set of mambos. They were, I swear, absolutely conical and gave one the impress—"

Bam! Blam!

Their waiter, arms outflung, ran from the kitchen, pursued by billows of smoke. "The chef's exploded! The chef's exploded!"

"That's too bad, he seemed a pretty good chef," remarked Palma, "judging from the food samples I've wiped off myself."

"I'll head out to the university tomorrow to see Ferrier," said Summer. "It's going to take you longer to make a trip to the border and back."

"I've checked with some people already. I can make it from here, through the fighting zone, to the border in a couple of days," said the photographer. "I should, if all goes well, return triumphantly to the capital in a week."

"If all goes well," said Summer.

CHAPTER 6

———◆———

"I hope this one don't go exploding," said Summer's steamcab driver.

The cab, with much chuffing and banging, was climbing the hill that led to the campus of King Waldo University. "Your cabs have a tendency to explode?" asked Summer, alone now.

"Last one surely did. Blew up twice, in point of fact, and me in it both times and once the Duchess of Westlake my passenger, and her toting a bushel basket of muskmelons. What a mess it did make."

The midday sky was a clear thin blue. The nearer they got to the university the more trees there were on each side of the broad road.

"Same thing happened to my horse," continued the driver.

"He exploded?"

"Into a million pieces, as the saying goes. Told them at the yard I didn't want a steamhorse, but they gave me a lot of folderol about making a gradual transition from horse-drawn cabs to steam-driven cabs and I, like the booby I oftimes am, went along. Well, sir, one moment I'm sitting in the driver's seat staring a robot horse square in the bung and then *Bam!*

Blam! he ups and explodes. And do you know who I happened to be hauling in my cab that day?"

"Not the Duchess of Westlake with more melons?"

"Nay, someone much more important than that, sir. It was none other than Princess Joline herself."

"She'd be ... the king's daughter?"

"That she would, the poor lass. No fun having a goofy dad. I know; my own pa was not all shipshape upstairs, a good deal bonkers he was. Rather a tough burden to bear, having your old pa tossed into St. Charlie's while you're hardly less than a lad."

"What's St. Charlie's?"

"Never heard of it, have you? Why, it's the St. Charles Public Lunatic Home. Wouldn't be a bit surprised if King Waldo himself didn't end up there."

"Figure he's the Phantom of the Fog?"

"No doubt about it, to my way of thinking. See him on the TV last night? 'I'm not a killer,' says he. Try to pin that in your cap. These are not the best of times ... what with the war and the king barmy. Enough to make a man ... Well, sir, here we are."

Viewed from the gilded entrance gates, the campus seemed to be all rolling hills and shady glades. Very few buildings were visible. Students there were, several hundred of them roaming the paths and byways. Just as Summer passed through the huge gates bells started chiming. In all the many trees birds took up their songs.

"Shoot, I'm going to get another headache." A slim green girl in a lycra singlet and shorts was standing beneath an oak which was especially thick with chirping bluebirds. She held several bookspools and a battered talkwriter pressed to her breasts.

Summer slowed. "Don't enjoy warbling?"

"Shoot, the singing isn't half so bad as the explosions," said the pretty green girl. "I usually try not to be aboveground when they're scheduled to go off, except today I was kept late in Soccer Appreciation. They're not real birds, you know, they're teenie-weenie steam robots. When they're not twittering they're—"

Pang!

A robot bird exploded directly above them. Blue feathers, cogs, twists of wire, and plastic eyes came dribbling down through the thick branches.

"Shoot, it's going to take me half an hour to comb this little tin bugger's innards out of my hair." She shook her head, dislodging most of the remains of the tiny robot. "You're too old to be a student, aren't you?"

"That I am," admitted Summer.

"Yet you're too rational seeming and aggressively masculine to be an instructor. What does that leave?"

"I'm a reporter. Right now I'm searching for Dr. Ferrier."

"Shoot, is he the cryptic one! I swear he has the most labyrinthine thought processes I've ever seen," said the girl. "Wouldn't you rather have an ice-cream soda at the malt shop?"

"I would, but at my age I must put duty first."

"Shoot. Well, you'll find Dr. Ferrier down in the Bio Wing, in Building Twenty-three-B. The entrance is by those oak trees on yonder hill. It's a shame, rather, to replace your sense of fun and adventure with a single-minded devotion to routine, but I suppose you know what you're doing." She smiled and left him.

"Shoot," murmured Summer as he climbed to the indicated entrance. There was an oval opening in the ground, showing a ramp that wound downward.

There was everything under here. Wide walkways, tranquil lagoons, steamswans, many-storied teaching buildings of neoglass and bright metal, bookspool-shops, soda fountains, cafeterias, burgerpits, at least three hospitals, tennis courts, airball fields, used steamcar dealers, robot repair shops. All lit, gently, with a crosshatch of floating lightstrips. The air was filtered and comfortable.

Near the entrance to building 23B a small rally, involving roughly a hundred students and six watching campus cops, was taking place.

"King Waldo is a killer!" a young catman in a candy-striped two-piece studysuit was shouting from the makeshift platform. "When fog-ridden night falls upon our great capital King Waldo dons the sinister garb which is now infamous across the length and breadth of the universe. He lurches forth, his mad-dened brain goading him to further bestial acts, and—"

"I don't wish to interrupt my opponent's flow of argument," cried a chunky lizard girl who'd jumped up from a chair on the platform. "Yet I am compelled to point out that his facts are all wrong. In the first place, King Waldo is not a killer. Secondly, he does not even own, let alone don as day deserts our fair capital, the garb which—"

"Lies! Propagandist lies!" said the catman youth.

Summer made his way up the ramp into 23B.

A very old robot, most likely an Earth System retread, sat at a lucite desk in the foyer. "How . . . how . . . can . . . we . . ." The words, having a rusty sound, came slowly out of the robot's mouth. "How can we . . ."

"Help me?"

"Yes, how can we help you, sir?"

"I'd like to see Dr. Ferrier."

Clang!

The robot had brought a hand up to his chest, harder than he'd intended apparently. He knocked himself off his lucite stool. "Would . . . would . . . you . . . be . . . would you be . . . would you be so kind as to . . ."

"Help you up?"

"Help me up, yes."

Summer lifted the dented old robot reception man back onto his perch. "You seemed unsettled by my mention of Dr. Ferrier. Is something wrong?"

"Oh . . . no . . . ha . . . ha . . . ha . . ." said the robot. "Nothing wrong . . . I was thinking . . . thinking of something else. Mind . . . often wanders . . . wanders off at . . . at my . . ."

"At your age?"

"Mind often wanders off at my age."

"As to Dr. Ferrier?"

"He's in . . ."

This time Summer couldn't supply the end to the robot's sentence. He waited.

"He's in . . . Who were we talking about?"

"Ferrier, Dr. Ferrier."

Clang!

"Easy there, you almost fell off again. How about

simply giving me the number of Dr. Ferrier's office?"

"Ah, yes. He's in office ... office three-oh-two. Our steam escalator ... unfortunately ... escalator unfortunately ... unfortunately ..."

"Exploded?"

"It exploded. You'll have to walk."

Summer walked up a purple ramp to the third floor. For some reason there was ivy growing in the corridor. It was all over the pale walls, twining around the light mobiles and voicegrids, clogging the water alcove.

Summer knocked at 302 and waited. He knocked again after a moment. A moment more and he went in.

A large man with an unevenly trimmed red beard was leaning, hands in pockets, against the bare wall of the bare room. "Sorry, I didn't hear your knock, pal." Summer got the impression the big man's voice was coming from someplace other than his mouth. "Can I help you?"

"I'd like to talk to Dr. Ferrier."

"Who might you be, pal?"

"Jack Summer."

"Not the same Jack Summer who writes those incisive articles for *Muckrake*?"

"Yeah, the same. You aren't Ferrier, are you?"

The red-bearded man shook his head. "Naw, I'm Dr. Alex Brownlove, Jr. Perhaps you've read my book, *Fun With Your Brain*?"

"I haven't, but I'm certain it's incisive. Is Ferrier around?"

"We have arrived at the sad part of the tale, pal." Brownlove ceased leaning, to come closer to Summer.

"It's a truly tragic thing. Dr. Ferrier has gone completely blooey in the head. He's completely coocoo, nuttier than a seedmuffin. We had to haul him away only a matter of hours ago. I'm here to gather up the last of his belongings."

"Where was he taken?"

"Anxious to interview him?"

"Nope, I'm on Peregrine to write up something on the Starbuck claimant," said Summer. "Ferrier has nothing to do with that. He happens to be a friend of my editor's, and I promised to look him up."

Grunting a little, Brownlove took his hands out of his pockets. He walked nearer, head cocked, eyes narrowed. "I hate to be the first to break this to you, Jack, old pal, but you don't look so very hot yourself." He tugged thoughtfully at his beard. "Wow, you look like you got a spell of wackiness coming on. I'd hate to think goofiness is contagious."

"It isn't. Where can I find Dr. Ferrier?"

"Yeah, see, you're getting obsessive, developing what we brain experts call one of these here now fixed ideas. A shame, too, a nice young guy like you all of a sudden going absolutely gaga."

"I'm not going—"

"Boys! I'm afraid we got us another one!"

From a back room of the office stepped three large-size catmen. Each wore a gray smock with St. Charles Public Lunatic Home stenciled on the breast pocket.

Summer started backing for the door.

All three of them were on him before he made it.

CHAPTER 7

———◆———

The blazing torch inscribed a wobbly arc across the afternoon, and landed with a sparkling splat square in the middle of the shingled church roof.

"Yippee, that's going to burn real good."

"Not going to fizzle out like the other ones."

"Hurry up and get that brick walkway ripped up. We'll bust some more windows."

"I get first try at the window with all the angels."

"Excuse me, gentlemen," said Palma, "merely passing through." He was mounted on a black stallion he'd rented several towns back. He attempted to guide the animal around the crowd of churchwreckers who were blocking the width of Louton's principal street.

"Wowee, here comes the preacher! Let's roll him in the muck!"

"Naw, let's roll him in shit!"

"Both, both. Muck *and* shit."

"Hey, yowee, let's shoot this stranger's horse."

"Gentlemen, this beast is the property of the Ace Stables in nearby—"

Bang!

The horse toppled over sideways, with Palma in the saddle. He kicked free of the stirrups, and rolled out from under before the dead stallion smacked the muddy street.

"Goody, did you see the look in his eye when the horse fell down?"

"Sort of surprised you, huh, Mr. Baldybean."

Palma brushed mud off himself, inspected the cameras hanging around his neck. He skirted the dead horse and walked up to the catman who'd shot it. "I have a terrific sense of humor," he said, smiling. "I'm noted throughout the galaxies for being receptive to all types of whimsy."

"Good enough, skinhead, then stick around," urged a lizardman. "We're going to roll the preacher in shit. That's always whimsical."

Palma ignored him, concentrating on the catman. "However, some things are not funny."

"Oh, yeah?"

"Take, for instance, setting a church on fire. That is not funny," the bald photographer continued. "Shooting my horse out from under me, to give you another example. That is not funny."

"Sure it—"

Palma suddenly jabbed a fist deep into the catman's middle. Before he could straighten up, Palma gave him two chops to the neck and then tripped him over. The catman splashed flat out in the mud and stayed there.

"That was funny," laughed the lizardman. "You got a keen sense of the absurd, cleanhead."

"Thank you." Palma bowed slightly at the crowd, stepped on the back of the sprawled catman and over to the sidewalk.

"I don't know if I think that's so funny," said a birdman. "Coldcocking Lloyd and stepping on him."

"Sure it was. That was hilarious."

"No, I got a mind to . . ."

Palma kept walking away from them. He was due to meet an informant at one of Louton's inns in a half hour.

When he passed the next alley a gob of green and orange feathers splashed out on him. Palma halted, peered.

" . . . You bumptious flapdoodler. I'll furl you up a gaffer's arsyvarsy! Then I'll—"

"You and who else, you doodledasher! I'll stow you in a phizgig's needlecase!"

"Ten smackers on Gentleman Jim," growled the catman nearest to Palma.

"Taken! Young Stribling can't be beat."

Craning his neck, Palma was able to see around the cluster of men in the alley and view what they were watching. It was a bird fight, between two disreputable foot-high talking parrots.

"You tunbellied beantosser," taunted Gentleman Jim through his blood-spattered beak.

"You're nothing but an elevated whoretwanger, my lad," rejoined Young Stribling, who was the one who'd lost the feathers.

Palma paused long enough to shoot half a roll of film. "*Sporting Life* may want to use one of these birds on their Athlete-of-the-Week page."

He met one of the waiters from the inn while he was still half a block from the place. The man, white apron flapping, came flying out of a second-floor window of the Eye & Finger Inn. Trailing bright bits of broken glass, he sailed through the air, to land with a jarring bounce directly in Palma's path.

"Darn, landed on the same side of my bum as last time." The waiter, a hefty bald man, got up with a helping hand from Palma. "This is not my lucky day. Most times I can twist some in midflight so as to land on different parts of myself. Today, I don't know why, I'm off." He stopped massaging his backside, to stare at the photographer. "God bless me, you're as hairless as I am."

"I noticed."

"You best stay away from the Eye and Finger, sir," warned the bald waiter. "There's a great ill-tempered lout in there, hairy as a mountain grout, and he can't abide the sight of a bare scalp."

"I've got business with the innkeeper. Is he in there?"

"One-Eye, you mean? Aye, he's ducked down behind the free lunch counter. This great hirsute lout is also threatening to clout anyone who's partially bald. One-Eye's hair has been getting a little thin lately so—"

"Thanks for the advice, even though I'm going to ignore it." Leaving the man standing there, Palma proceeded up to the thick oaken doors of the inn. The painted sign of the Eye & Finger showed a calloused forefinger being thrust into a moderately bloodshot eye, apparently commemorating the incident in which the innkeeper earned his nickname.

The first customer Palma encountered inside the place was sitting uneasily at a table and feeling the top of his head. "You wouldn't say I was bald, would you? I mean to say, there's quite a bit of fuzz all over here and around the ears; just feel, you'll find considerable growth.... Good gad! Turn around, my friend, and feel! There's no way you can pass for hairy."

"I appreciate your timely warning. However—"

"Hair and balls!" roared a voice from above. "Them as has one has the other! Them as don't, don't!"

Palma wended his way among the tables, which were all round and oaken. About half of the patrons of this level of the inn were in various stages of ducking and departing.

A pretty serving girl with a very interesting bosom stood at the foot of the stairway leading upward. She was holding a copper serving tray as a shield.

"That appears to be a fairly substantial tray, miss."

"Oh ... oh ... yes ... it's very substantial," answered the girl.

"No hair, no nuts!" boomed the baldness-hating customer above. "Show me a baldy, I'll show you a sissy!"

"Allow me to borrow your tray for a moment, miss." Palma slid it out of her grasp and hefted it.

"Oh ... oh ... I feel defenseless."

"No need; Palma is here to champion your—"

"By the saints!" exclaimed the girl, noticing the top of his head for the first time. "It's no hair you have!"

"Not a bit, no."

"Then that shaggy brute up there will do with you what he's done with three waiters, five customers, and a visiting male nurse. That is to say he'll—"

"Nothing to fear." Tray under his arm, Palma mounted the wooden stairs to the second-floor dining room.

All the tables were overturned. Green bottles, gold-tinted bottles, sky-blue bottles were smashed to bits on the plank flooring. Bowls of gravy, a stuffed pig, loaves of black bread, and several tossed green salads had been scattered hither and yon. A bald-headed old man lay unconscious with his pale face resting on a fat round cheese.

The hairy man had his back to Palma. He was throttling a hairless patron, shaking him violently as he did. His shoulder-length hair flapped at his shaggy bare back. "Hairy is good, baldy is bad," he was chanting.

Palma approached him carefully, avoiding several scattered bunches of purple grapes and a pool of white wine that originated at the overturned gallon jug on the hairy man's table.

Clong!

"Glory be! What manner of—"

Clong!

The second whack over the head caused the hairy man to let go of his victim, stagger and slump to his knees.

Clong! Clong!

The hairy man fell forward into a tureen.

Resting the borrowed tray against a tipped table, Palma walked to the row of broken windows to survey the street below. "Fore," he called out.

He rolled the hairy man, who felt to weigh about two hundred and fifty pounds, over to the newly made opening and pushed him out.

"Oh, sir, it's a hero you are!" The serving girl had ventured up to watch the conflict. "Never in all my days have I seen such courage, such bravery, in the face of frightening odds."

Palma wiped perspiration from his bald head with a table napkin. "What time do you get off?"

"Beg pardon, sir?"

"When do you get off work here?"

The girl frowned. "I don't at all, sir, seeing as how I'm an indentured servant of Mr. One-Eye Dodgson. I'm obliged to remain on the premises virtually around the clock."

"I'll talk to One-Eye about that. Then perhaps you'll allow me to escort you someplace for a quiet dinner."

"Oh, that would be most pleasant, sir. Though I doubt one can find a quiet dining place in Louton. The best we can hope for is one less raucous than this."

"That will suffice."

The innkeeper asked, "Have I told you how I lost my eye, Palma?"

"Yes." They were in the office of the Eye & Finger, a dim, windowless, dark-wood room. Palma sat in a tufted chair facing One-Eye Dodgson, who was hunched behind a carved desk.

"The proudest day of my life it was," One-Eye went on. "I don't know if I can convey to you in words the thrill of having one's eye gouged out for one's beloved country. It was three, no, four wars back and I—"

"Tully Keep," said Palma. "You're supposed to be setting up a meet. My contacts have already paid you for the job."

"Job's done, too, sir," said the innkeeper. "You're to meet an agent of Keep's in the village of Ravenshoe three days hence. Ravenshoe's a hundred long miles from here, and the only way you can reach it, in these war-torn times, is via stagecoach. It's the same in all wars, the delays and inconveniences. Take the day I gave my eye to the greater glory of my native territory. The day dawned fair, with only a breath of—"

"Who's Keep's agent? Where do I meet him?"

"He'll find you once you arrive in Ravenshoe and take a room at the Boot and Knee Inn," said One-Eye. "Place is owned and operated by that braggart Cock-foster, who thinks getting kicked in the kneecap on the battlefield is the same as having one's eye—"

"You've got a girl working here, a blond."

The innkeeper's sole eye narrowed. "She's a sweet and innocent flower, Palma. A delicate blossom struggling to bloom amid—"

"Save the horticultural allusions, I only want to take her to dinner," said Palma. "I'd appreciate your giving her some time off this evening."

"Palma, the child is learning a trade; every minute away from this establishment means a loss of precious opportunity for—"

"I'll tell her she can take the night off, commencing at six." Palma stood up.

Finally One-Eye nodded consent. "Remember she's a fragile bloom."

"I'll remember," Palma assured him.

CHAPTER 8

———————◆———————

The catman sneezed. A substantial sneeze which shook his large dappled body, caused his bowler hat to give a hop, and rattled the entire interior of the stagecoach. "Ah, nothing like it, sir." Giving a contented sigh, he dipped a furry thumb and forefinger again into his silver snuffbox. This pinch of snuff he inserted into his other nostril. "May I offer you a bit of my special blend, sir? It's made up for ... ah ... ah ... ah ... ahchoo!"

Palma, seated across from the bulky catman, held on to his seat. The ordinary bouncing and swaying of their progress along the dusty road he was just about used to. "No thanks."

"Snuff, sir," said the catman while stuffing the silver box into a vest pocket and brushing specks from his trousers and coat, "snuff is the universal curative. Would you believe I have not had so much as a touch of the gout since I became a user of the miraculous stuff? Nay, nor have I suffered with the grippe, the quincy, brain fever, or the vapors. I venture to say snuff might well put curly locks back on that gleaming pate of yours, sir."

"So would a wig." Palma settled back in the seat. He and the snuff-dipping catman were the only pas-

sengers on the jolting morning coach. There was
woodland unreeling outside, tall trees and shady
brush cut across by stripes of sunlight.

"You'll forgive me for suggesting, sir, that you and I
may share an interest in common."

Palma touched one of his dangling cameras. "You
take pictures as a hobby?"

The catman chuckled. His chuckle shook the coach
nearly as much as his sneezes. "Nay, sir, I am no tink-
erer with gadgets. At Silcotes Hall, my ancestral
home, I have steadfastly refused to allow this and
that new mechanism to be installed," he said. "I was
alluding, sir, to a probable shared interest in paps."

"Huh?"

"I refer, sir, to bubbies. Or what are more com-
monly known as butterbags, charlies, dugs, poonts,
and cabman's rests."

"Oh, you mean tits?"

"Precisely, sir," said the catman, chuckling and
wheezing. "When you bade a forlorn farewell to the
amply founted serving wench at the Eye and Finger I
could not help but notice the way you gazed at her
blubbers, sir."

Palma rubbed at the top of his head. "I guess you
might say I'm something of a fount fan ... but I don't
like to be the sort of chap who brags about his lady
acquaintances."

The catman had turned to watch the forest. "I do
hope we don't encounter them," he muttered. "Now,
sir, let us continue our pleasant discussion of mam-
mies."

"Who is *them*?"

Making a dismissing gesture, the catman said, "Too

early in the day to worry about them, sir. . . . I can understand your reluctance to talk of your most recent affair of the heart. Surely, however, after the passage of time one is not—"

"I'm wondering about *them*," Palma told him. "Before we get to my Life and Loves, explain."

"Surely, sir, you're aware we're traveling through country that is notorious for the number of highwaymen per square mile."

"Highwaymen?"

"Indeed, sir, highwaymen. This forest, dubbed Cutpurse Wood by the local wits, is often crawling with them. I do believe it is a bit early in the day to attract them, which is why I invariably make it a habit whenever I travel away from Silcotes Hall to patronize the most daylight-surrounded coach available."

Palma half stood to gaze out the window. "I hadn't heard about the highwaymen."

"Full many a famed rascal haunts Cutpurse Wood, sir." He took out his silver snuffbox to fondle as he spoke. "There's the infamous Jonathan Hawkes; there was, until he was captured and publicly drawn and quartered, Captain Hardcastle; there is the brutal Squinteye Jim; there's the ruthless Scarlet Angel; there is—"

"That's a sort of feminine name for a highwayman—the Scarlet Angel. Is he perhaps a little bit—"

"The Scarlet Angel is a woman, sir."

"Oh, so?"

"Such a woman as would appeal to butterbag fanciers such as ourselves," amplified his fellow passenger. "It is said she's no more than five and twenty years of age, sir, and that her poonts are most marvelous in both breadth and—"

Bang!

"Yowl"

Bam! Bang!

Palma stood up so fast his head clunked on the coach ceiling. "Hey, somebody just shot our driver clean off his perch."

"Whoa! Stop where you are, you moth-ridden nags!" the catman shouted.

The stage came to a clattering stop.

"I very much fear, sir, that we have fallen into the hands of brigands of the road." He swallowed, then ran his prickly tongue over his lips. Hurriedly he tucked the snuffbox away. "I'll venture to reconnoiter ... By Godfrey, it's the lot of them! There is the infamous Jonathan Hawkes, the brutal Squinteye Jim, and the ruthless Scarlet Angel."

"The Scarlet Angel." Palma stuck his bald head out into the bright woodland morning. "Rumors about her tremendous knockers are true, too true."

"Get that winter melon of a cabeza back inside there, mate!" ordered Squinteye Jim with a wave of one of his blaster pistols.

"You must be the fabled Squinteye Jim." Palma did not withdraw his head. "The very man I am seeking. I'm Palma, the famed photographer, and I've been sent to Cutpurse Wood for the purpose of capturing your visage on film for the pages of *Front Page Detective* Magazine and—"

"Back in the stage, melonhead, or you've breathed your last!" Squinteye Jim aimed his pistol.

Palma pulled back. "We'd also like a few candid

shots of Jonathan Hawkes," he called out into the morning. "Casual stuff, possibly of your burying a sack of loot or—"

"Do you not wish my picture as well?" The Scarlet Angel had dismounted and came to his window. She was a lovely red-haired girl, wearing a green tunic, green riding pants and boots. Two pistols were buckled around her slim waist.

"I don't know," said Palma, eyeing her. "You might tell me who you are and I can check the list of cutthroats, highwaymen, and bravos that *Front Page Detective* gave me."

Her green eyes went wide. "Why, I am the Scarlet Angel. Surely I am known to you by reputation?"

Palma eased a sheet of paper out of a tunic pocket, pretended to consult it. "Let's see ... Scarface Ned, Springheel Jack, Surly Mac, the Terrible Turk. Nope, don't seem to have any Scarlet Angel here, miss. What do you do?"

"Do?" She drew both pistols, thrust them under his nose. "You great blabbering ninny, I'm a highwayperson. I'm the Scarlet Angel. Renowned far and wide."

Palma tucked away the alleged list. "I'm from out of town," he said. "There are degrees of far and wide. Someone may be a somebody right around his hometown, but—"

"You've heard of Jim and Jonathan."

"Sure, they're notorious."

"I'm as notorious as they are."

"Enough gab, mates." Squinteye Jim, his left eye narrowed nearly shut, jerked open the opposite door to grab the catman. "We've got all the goods off the top. Now, let's have a look at you, you feline Midas."

"Me, sir? I am but a poor circuit-riding minister of the Church of the—"

"You're Silcote of Silcotes," Squinteye Jim told him, "and carrying a money belt packed with gold around your fat middle."

"I may be a bit overweight, sir, but it is from an overfondness for hot buttered scones and not because—"

"Out with you!" Squinteye Jim pulled Silcote completely out of the stage and dumped him into the roadside brush.

"You're not a bad-looking girl," Palma said to the Scarlet Angel. "Too many freckles, though some of our readers might go for that splotched effect."

"Too many! You blabbering booby, my freckles are my best feature. Many's the man, and some of them of very high station, who's raved about the very freckles you have scorned. No doubt you've heard of Richard Ferncourt Allen, who was Poet Laureate of Laranja East five years running. It was specifically for me that he composed his touching poem, 'To His Freckled Shepherdess.'"

"You used to be a shepherdess?"

"Nay, but Richard had a commission to turn out a half dozen pastoral lyrics that season."

"Hey there! Slit his gizzard and get it over with, Angel." This was a new voice, deep and cruel.

"In a moment, Johnny, shortly."

"Ha! Feast your eyes on these gold Waldos, Johnny my lad!" roared Squinteye Jim. "This tub of a Silcote is infested with coins."

"Relieve him of them swiftly," ordered Hawkes in

his harsh voice, "and sink your dirk into his fuzzy car-
cass."

"Oh, sir," pleaded Silcote, "I would much prefer to
remain among the living. Suppose I arrange for you
to be given another bag of golden Waldos?"

"Arrange for me to swing from the gallows tree you
mean."

To the lovely Scarlet Angel Palma said, "I have the
idea you'd be just right for our *Brides* Magazine.
Yeah, I can see you in a tasteful two-page spread de-
murely dressed in white—"

"Would I not have to be wed to appear in *Brides?*"

"Not essential. What's important is that fresh, innocent glow you so obviously possess."

"I have tried to retain my innocence in the face of
great odds," said the redhead.

"Ho!" exclaimed Squinteye Jim. "Here's another
money pouch hidden in his armpit, and this one bulg-
ing with silver Jolines."

"I do wish you'd spare those, sir. They're the
proceeds from the Benefit Barn Sale for the Lame and
Halt Veterans of the—"

"Kill him first, then search him," suggested Hawkes.
"It will spare us all this gab."

"Too bad I won't be able to photograph you," said
Palma.

"Why not?" She tapped a camera with the barrel of
one of her pistols. "You have all the necessary equipment."

"The big stumbling block, Angel, is my forthcoming
demise."

"Oh, I can talk them out of killing you. They owe

me a favor for letting them keep the girl scouts from the picnic we raided last month."

Palma grinned. "I'd appreciate your interceding," he said. "Might I ask one more small favor?"

"You have but to put it into words."

"My traveling companion, Squire Silcote, is an essential part of my crew," said Palma. "He holds various pieces of gear, is an expert on lighting."

"Surely Squinteye could hold your things."

"I don't like to dwell on a man's handicaps, Angel, but I need an assistant with keen vision. A guy who's earned the nickname Squinteye doesn't sound as though—"

The girl said, "Jonathan would never help you, so I guess we'll have to spare the squire." She walked around the coach.

Squinteye Jim drew out a blood-caked knife from his leather belt. "Prepare to meet—"

"Hold," said the Scarlet Angel.

"What?"

"I wish him alive."

"Gnats! I'm blowed if I'll—"

"He is to live." The girl pointed both the pistols at Squinteye Jim.

"But I've worked myself up to pigsticking this bloke, girl."

"Gather up the money and stand aside, Squint, else I'll fry your liver and lights."

"Here now, Angel! What's all this?" Hawkes strode up to them, a giant man and a good half of him metal. His right arm was aluminum, the top of his head copper, his right leg from the knee down stainless steel. The kilt outfit he favored revealed most of his metallic additions and substitutions.

"I want the hairless one and this one," the girl told him.

"What for?"

"You've no reason to question and nag at me, Johnny. I want them both, that's it."

Hawkes rubbed his flesh fingers along his silvery arm. "You know I never tire of doing you favors, Angel, and yet—"

"Load up this morning's takings, and let's have no more arguing," she said.

"Very well." Hawkes gave a brief nod, then walked to his horse.

Palma let out his breath, wiped the sweat from his scalp, and climbed out of the stage.

Squinteye Jim laughed. "If you tire of them as swiftly as you've tired of all the rest, Angel," he said, "I'll have the pleasure of slicing them both up before long."

A few moments later they were all ready to depart. With Palma mounted on one of the freed coach horses and the squire on another the party rode away along a forest bypath.

"Don't let Squint's remarks unsettle you," said the girl, who rode alongside Palma. "I'm not so fickle as—"

Bam! Blam!

"The coach." Palma looked back. Black smoke was rolling through the forest from the place where they'd left the stage. "Why'd you folks fix it to blow up?"

The Scarlet Angel shook her head. "But we didn't,"

she said. "The bomb must have been in there all along, set to go off at this exact moment."

"Oy," said Palma, realizing what that meant. "Then someone wanted to get rid of me . . . or the squire."

The redhead reached over and took his hand. "It was indeed fate which brought us together. Had I not stopped your coach and decided to take you with me, you'd be nothing but debris now."

"Oy," repeated Palma.

CHAPTER 9

———◆———

Dr. Brownlove circled the white table. "Before I continue this morning's lecture I would like to remind you gentlemen it's an honor to be chosen for the King's Commandos," he said. "Isn't that so, Mr. Beesant?"

Up in the third tier of seats a young birdman with blue plumage suddenly sat upright. "What, sir?"

"I was saying, Mr. Beesant, that a King's Commando must be alert and ever watchful. You'd agree with that, pal?"

"Ah, indeed, truly, yes, Dr. Brownlove," replied the commando cadet.

"I'm glad you are in agreement with me." The shaggy doctor made another full circle of the brightly illuminated white table. "Being alert and watchful, Mr. Beesant, you no doubt heard the last scream of pain our morning's subject emitted."

"Oh, yes, sir, I did, surely, Dr. Brownlove. Scream fair gave me the whim-whams."

"Will you tell the class how that whim-wham-producing scream was elicited from our subject?"

"Um . . ." Beesant scratched at the feathers atop his head. "It is somewhat difficult to see clearly from up

61

here.... Um ... I think you coshed him in his nut-
megs, sir."

"How's that again?" Dr. Brownlove cupped a hand
to his ear. "Please, gentlemen, do not prompt alert
and watchful Mr. Beesant."

A few of the hundred other commando cadets had
whispered to the blue-plumed youth.

"I mean his codlings, sir. His knackers. You know,
the chap's balls."

"Close, Mr. Beesant. However ..." Brownlove
stepped closer to the white table and drove two fingers into a spot just below Summer's ribs. "Could you
see that clearly, Mr. Beesant? Not the knackers at all,
was it? Yes, Mr. LeMond?"

"How come the chappy didn't howl in agony this
time, sir?"

"Good question, pal." Brownlove bent over Summer. "The reason is simple. He's passed out cold." The
doctor turned his back on Summer and scanned the
audience which circled him. "What's our next likely
step? Suppose we'd been questioning this idiot and he
conked out on us before we got all the info we
wanted. What then?"

"Sir, sir!"

"Here, sir, here!"

"I've the answer!"

Brownlove stroked his beard. "Mr. Abel seems most
eager to answer. Perhaps his recent nap has improved
his thinking processes. Answer if you please, Mr.
Abel."

"I wasn't dozing, sir," protested the lizard lad. "I've
been poised here, lapping up every word, every de-
tail, every gem of—"

"We await an answer, Mr. Abel."

"Yes, the answer. Well, what I'd do is give him a touch of the shockstick right in the old jewelcase, sir."

"Where, Mr. Abel?"

"In the marblebag, sir. You know, in the fellow's balls."

"Ah, yes. Excellent suggestion." From an array of instruments on a white stand next to the table on which Summer was strapped he selected a thin silver rod. "This one should do the job."

Summer groaned. The soggy rat that had been inspecting his bloody right hand scurried into a murky corner of the small stone room. The reporter groaned once more, made a yawning, gasping inhalation. He'd been dropped in a puddle of scummy water. After considerable effort he elbowed and rolled to a drier spot on the stone floor of his cell. They'd put his clothes back on him while he was unconscious, and parts of cloth were sticking to the raw and bloody spots on his body.

Summer sat up finally. He couldn't remember how many of his fingernails were gone. Not worth checking right now. He left his hands resting on his knees. "St. Charlie's," he said aloud.

The various locks on his cell door squeaked and rasped.

Summer stayed where he was. This time they could carry him wherever they wanted him.

A long-legged, willowy blond girl in a spotless off-white singlet and slacks entered. "Oh, you poor man, sitting right on the floor instead of on your nice wooden stool."

"I usually sprawl on the floor after being tortured. And who the hell are you?"

The door was closed behind the blond girl. "Is that one of the symptoms of your madness? Do you have the notion people have been torturing you?"

"Notion?" He held out his bloody hands toward her. "What do you think these are . . . stigmata?"

"You probably hurt yourself while thrashing around on the floor. Are you subject to fits?"

"I'm going to be shortly. Who are you?"

"Why, don't you recognize me, you poor unfortunate wretch? I'm your princess."

"You mean the one I've been dreaming of since boyhood?"

"No, no, I'm Princess Joline. King Waldo's only daughter. Surely you're enough in touch with reality to recog—"

"Why are you here?"

"I visit St. Charlie's every other day to work among the unfortunate wrecks," explained the princess. "You're, by the way, quite good looking for a lunatic."

"Princess, you've got to get to your father's Minister of Propaganda. Tell him Jack Summer of *Muckrake* is being held—"

"Is that who you think you are? Ah, would that you truly were, since I have long admired the courageous work of Jack Summer, the incisive—"

"I am Jack Summer." He managed to rise to his feet. "They've taken all my stuff, otherwise I could show you my ID packet."

"Now, it's best not to excite yourself." She held out a steadying hand, which kept him from toppling over into her.

"You said you read *Muckrake*?"

"Of course I do. My father, the king, allows me to subscribe, at the teleport rate even, though he feels—"

"Back issues. Have any?"

"I keep a stack of them under my royal bed. A maid of mine chides me for—"

"Go home, thumb through them, find the contributors page. You'll see my—"

"All things going oaky-doaky in here, your highness?" A large lizardman had opened the door and was scowling into the cell.

"Yes, Osbert. I'm on the point of leaving."

Summer said, "Will you—"

"I have to move on to the next lunatic; my bodyguard's growing impatient," said Princess Joline. She helped him lean against the wall so he wouldn't fall over when she took her hand away. "I won't forget your case, you have my word."

CHAPTER 10

The sound of thunder came rolling across the plain; a hot wind shook the high yellow grass.

"Yike!"

"Ah, forgive me," apologized the Scarlet Angel. "Thunder and lightning are among the few things I fear in this world. Whenever I hear the ominous boom of thunder I grab hold of someone for protection." The lovely red-haired girl was leaning far out of her saddle, clutching Palma.

"Your motive doesn't bother me," said the photographer in a strained voice. "What unsettles me is that you've grabbed me in an intimate spot."

The Scarlet Angel relaxed her grip. "Again I must beg your forgiveness, dear Palma," she said. "Little did I realize I'd clutched your bushwhacker in my fright."

Palma exhaled, saying, "Took me by surprise is all. Not that I . . . Yow!"

The thunder rumbled closer.

The girl tightened her hold on him. "Dear me, have I made another assault on your quimstake?"

Palma nodded.

"I assure you I am not, despite my reputation as a hellion and highwayperson, the sort who makes a habit of laying hold of a gentleman's tickletoby."

"I'm not exactly a gentleman."

"Even so, it was thoughtless of me to allow my own fright to cause discomfort to your wagstaff."

Rain, hot and sticky, commenced pouring down out of the yellow-gray afternoon sky.

"Let's urge some speed out of these nags," said Jonathan Hawkes, who rode at the head of the party. "Rain plays bloody havoc with my spare parts."

The Scarlet Angel let go of Palma completely, spurring her mount. "Come along, we must protect your sweet hairless head from the ravages of this storm."

The rain roared down as they galloped, sizzling lightning-scribbled zigzags across sheets of it. After a few wet and windy minutes they were across the plain and into a woodland area. They soon reached a clearing in which stood a small forlorn wood-and-plaster inn. The flapping sign over the oaken door gave the place's name as the Knuckle & Chin Inn.

"Ah, the Knuckle and Chin," observed Silcote. "I've heard of the place, though I believed the war had shut its doors."

"There was considerable fighting through here some weeks since," said Squinteye Jim, "causing the good boniface to flee with his cash and kin. He's not soon likely to return, which is why we're residing herein. Now, let us quickly stable these steeds."

They were met in the main dining room of the Knuckle & Chin by a bent old man barely five feet high. "You didn't warn me we'd be having guests," he said to Squinteye Jim. "You know I like to fix soup and salad when—"

"Enough blab," said Hawkes. "These two lads are

to be locked in the servants' room and fed on stale bread and water."

The old man rubbed his hands anxiously on his apron. "I'm clean out of stale bread, Jonathan. The best I can do is day-old scones or—"

"I care not a fig what you feed them," boomed the cyborg highwayman, "so long as they are locked away out of my sight."

"Figs," murmured the old man. "We have a whole sack of figs. Mayhap I could whip up a puddi—"

"Away with both of them!"

The Scarlet Angel, nostrils flaring wide, placed herself directly in front of Hawkes. "There'll be no locking up and no stale bread while—"

"How about two-day-old muffins?" asked the old man.

"By glory!" cried Hawkes, shaking his metal fist at the girl. "I spared these two wretches, Angel, but I'll be—"

"They'll have one of the guest rooms," she told him evenly. "They'll dine with us or—"

"Speaking of food," said Squinteye Jim, "what's for lunch, Fireball?"

The old man unbent slightly, chuckling. "I've got grout stew simmering in the kitchen, Squint. Made with fresh turnips, diced onions, zabinga leaves, a touch of—"

"Ho!" exclaimed the catman suddenly. "Can this old gentleman I see before me be none other than Captain Fireball?"

Fireball's head bobbed. "Perhaps you were an admirer of mine during my heyday, sir? I was the best-known and, I have to admit, the best-loved highwayman of my generation. The pamphlets and books they wrote of me numbered in the hundreds. One of them, *A Narrative of the Remarkable Life of the Notorious Captain Fireball, Giving an Exact Description of His Robberies, Escapes, etc. and Based on Previously Unknown Facts*, was on the *Laranja Times Literary Supplement*'s Bestseller list for eighteen weeks in a row."

Spong!

Hawkes had slammed his aluminum fist against a wooden ceiling-support post. "I want no more badinage," he shouted. "Fireball, you doddering mumblecrust, I'll have my meal in the master suite. Angel, join me."

"Nay." She shook her red-head. "I must look after my guests, Johnny."

The flesh part of the huge robber's face flushed. "So be it!" Spinning on his metal leg he went thumping up a wooden staircase.

"There are quarrels in the best of households," said the old highwayman. "Make yourselves comfortable while I prepare the repast."

Squinteye poked the squire on the elbow. "You look to be a bloke with some taste."

Silcote answered, "In my own small way, sir, I—"

"I'll show you my collection, then."

"Collection, sir?"

"I'm not in this game merely for the cash," said Squinteye Jim. "I am also a hobbyist. Do you know what I collect?"

"I cannot venture to guess."

"Snuffboxes."

"Indeed, sir?" The catman pressed a paw to his vest pocket. "How many of them have you?"

"Nine hundred and seven to date, and each one has a story related to it." He gave the squire another nudge. "You'll enjoy looking at them, I wager."

"Yes, sir, of course."

When the two were gone the Scarlet Angel said, "Squint is the more understanding of my two comrades of the road. He sensed I wanted to be alone with you, sweet Palma."

"Understanding? He's the one who wants to slice away portions of me."

"He has a vicious side, but he's a deal more accommodating than Johnny." She seated herself on a window bench beneath a leaded window. "Join me."

Palma sat. "I get the impression you and Hawkes—"

"You know how it is when people work side by side." She stroked his head, rubbing away raindrops. "Friendships are bound to develop."

"Throats are bound to get cut."

"Johnny won't harm you, long as he knows I care for you," the Scarlet Angel assured him. "So you need not—"

"Yowl!"

Thunder had whammed in the courtyard, shaking the windows.

"Forgive me, I seem to have, in my unreasoning fear, clutched your gullyraker yet again."

Palma scanned the dining room. "Do you have a room of your own, Angel?"

"Yes, I do, dear Palma."

"It has, I trust, a door and a lock?"

"Oh, yes."

"Let's go there."

CHAPTER 11

———◆———

"They've left him to rot," said the thin catman. "Same as they left me to rot. They left Clark to rot, and he rotted. They left Estling to rot, and he rotted. They left Ruyle to—"

"Ruyle didn't rot," interrupted the white-bearded man in the corner. "He hanged himself with his suspenders. You're thinking of Wollter. *He* rotted."

"Ruyle *tried* to hang himself with his suspenders," said the catman. "But his suspenders were too elastic and he succeeded only in bouncing up and down between the rafter and the floor. They cut him down, and eventually he rotted. You're getting fuzzy in the upstairs, Dr. Yach."

"Perhaps I am. God bless the king!"

"You're doing pretty well today," a bright-haired young man said to Summer. "You're able to crawl and stumble unaided. That's not bad after all those sessions in the Torture Department."

Summer was on the floor of a cell. It didn't feel like his own. "Did you guys move in with me?" he said, voice a little quavery.

"Other way around; they tossed you in here with us."

The catman shuffled nearer. "Left you to rot," he

71

explained. "Same as Manzano, who was left here to rot and he rotted. Or take the case of Dugas, they left him here to rot and he rotted."

"You're too gloomy, Hesslin," complained Dr. Yach. "Of all the people I've shared this hole with during my eighteen years of unjust imprisonment in St. Charlie's you are the most gloomy."

"Come now, Doctor. I'm no more gloomy than Mossbarger."

"True, Mossbarger was quite gloomy. I'd forgotten him."

"Your once noble mind is on the skids, Doc."

"Perhaps so. God bless the king!"

The bright-haired young man asked, "Would you like me to help you sit up?"

"Sure, I might as well."

"My name is Angus Hare." He aided Summer into a sitting position against one of the cell's stone walls.

"Pleased to meet you. I'm Jack Summer."

"Yes, I know." Hare smiled and frowned at the same time. "You really are pleased to meet me?"

"I'm not clapping my hands and shouting whoopee, but I'm not saddened by the encounter either."

"Well, you have a much grander nature than I expected," said young Hare. "I suppose you've become used, hearing so much of it, to criticism. So that you're not touched by what I've been saying about you in *The People's Trumpet of Truth-Kings Must Die Weekly Sun.*"

"What have you been saying?"

The young man blinked. "I'm Angus Hare."

"That part I comprehend. I wasn't, though, aware you—"

"Ah, I see, Mr. Summer, you're pretending not to have read my reviews of your work. No doubt it helps you to avoid the deep hurts of having all your faults and inadequacies as a writer exposed to public scrutiny."

"I suppose it would," said Summer. "What I'm trying to tell you is I've never read your paper, or your reviews."

"That hardly seems likely, Mr. Summer. We faithfully sent two copies of each of my reviews to *Muckrake*. Surely—"

"Why did they move me into this cell?" Summer asked Hesslin.

"So you can rot."

"Could you give me a few more details?"

Dr. Yach said, "They're no doubt through experimenting with you. You've been dumped here, therefore. Here you'll stay."

"Somebody's bound to come looking for me," said Summer.

"There are no easily accessible records of this wing of St. Charlie's," said the bearded old man. "Anyone inquiring for you will be told either that you died or that you were discharged and they have no idea where you went thereafter."

"That won't work. My—"

"It's worked in my case. I was put here eighteen years ago because I firmly believed ... God bless the king! ... that a monarchy was best for Laranja East. A dangerous idea to advocate openly in those days."

"Laranja East *is* a monarchy."

"Now, yes." Dr. Yach nodded sadly. "I'm no longer

dangerous, but unfortunately I'm forgotten. I doubt I'll ever leave this room."

"Who is being gloomy now?" said Hesslin.

"You must have seen my review of your exposé of the Neptune situations," said young Hare. " 'Another Mediocre Mess of Reportage from the Barnum System's Most Overrated So-called Muckraker' was the title of the review."

"A catchy title, but I missed it." Summer folded his hands over one knee. "There must be a grapevine in St. Charlie's, if it's like most institutions. So news can get around, and outside."

"We have ways of finding out what's happening inside the walls," said the catman. "Getting any word out is nigh impossible."

"Thinker brings us inside news and carries messages," said Dr. Yach.

"Thinker?"

"A robot," sneered Hare. "Not a very efficient one either. Runs on steam, which as anyone knows is—"

"Thinker's been a dear friend to me since you were in rompers," said Dr. Yach. "He's the robot who brings our meals, Mr. Summer. Like myself, he was meant for better things and has been left to waste away in the bowels of St. Charlie's."

"I never wore rompers," said Hare. "Whatever they might be."

"I'm trying to locate Dr. Ferrier," Summer told them. "Is he in St. Charlie's?"

"Right you are," said Hesslin. "They've got him."

"Where is he?"

"Right here on subfloor four. They tossed him down here to rot."

"I'm assuming that, like us, Dr. Ferrier is not crazy," said Summer.

"Not at all," said the bearded old man. "It seems he is, however, dangerous to the present government. I wonder sometimes if even a monarchy is—"

"Dangerous how?"

"We don't have many details," said the catman. "Thinker has a hunch Dr. Ferrier is in St. Charlie's because of something he invented."

Summer looked across at the thick door. "Something he invented . . . how the hell does that tie in?"

"How's that again?" asked the doctor.

"Nothing." Summer was still watching the door. "I'm still a little vague on time. Think I passed out a few times. How long have I been bunking with you?"

"Three days," replied Hare.

"Three days? Then she's not going to do anything."

"Who?"

"Nobody," said Summer.

CHAPTER 12

At dawn Palma, naked and wide awake, got up off the edge of the wide feather bed where he'd been sitting. He padded across the beam-ceilinged bedroom, pushed the shutters open to stare out at the new day. "What a worthless lout you are," he told himself aloud.

The five cream-colored doves that were roosting on the thatch roof went fluttering up into the air.

"Here you are a mature adult grown-up," continued Palma as he leaned out the window to see if there was any sign of the Scarlet Angel's returning, "and once again, you've allowed yourself to be sidetracked. What folly. The first pair of extraordinary knockers that comes down the pike and you drop your assignment. Let your loyal chum, Jack Summer, down while you frolic with a highwayperson."

Palma scratched his backside, then wandered to the bed again. "Observe yourself, you miserable cur, waiting around for Angel to get home from work. She's turned you, she and her momentous gazoos, into some kind of suburban housewife. Fie and for shame. Here you've been for two days simply screwing your brains out while ... no, it's been three days." He held up a hand and started to tick off days on his fingers. "Let's see. I first slipped her the old sausage the afternoon we arrived here at the Knuckle and Chin. Then I exercised the old salami again after dinner that night and once again around about midnight. So that's one day. Then as day was breaking the next—"

"Adorable Palma!" The bedroom door swung open. The Scarlet Angel, fully clothed and wearing her riding boots, came striding in. She carried a burlap sack over her shoulder.

"I didn't hear your horses."

"We approached the stable by the rear roadway, dearest one," she said. "Did you pine for me as much as I for you?"

"I'm glad you brought this up, Angel, since I—"

"What loot we did acquire this night, beautiful Palma!" Thumping the heavy sack to the floor, she clapped her hands. "Come, feast your adorable eyes on it."

"Probably pretty much like yesterday's loot." He remained seated on the bed.

"I sometimes fear you take no real interest in my career, beloved Palma."

"It's not that, Angel. But, however, I do—"

"Is this not a prize?" She held up a gold cup. "Solid gold, encrusted with rare gems."

"How'd somebody happen to be carrying that around after dark?"

" 'Tis a trophy won by the Cutpurse Wood Field Hockey Team. They were carrying it home from a victorious game when we waylaid their coach."

"Oh, then that little gold guy on top is carrying a hockey stick."

"Actually it's a scythe. The trophy maker was all

out of hockey players and had to substitute a farmer left over from a Grange—"

"Angel, we really must have a—"

"And what of this treasure?" She laughed as he took a two-foot-high marble statue with a gold clock in its stomach from the loot bag.

"Yeah, I knew a girl like that once." The bald photographer decided he could better present his decision to move out of here if he had on his clothes.

"Here we have a sack of gold Waldos." She rattled the pouch, then thrust a hand in. "Look at this particular one. It's the rare minting where they left off half of King Waldo's moustache. A coin buff will pay upwards—"

"Angel, listen." Palma got into his allseason underwear. "There comes a moment in the affairs of men when love and duty—"

"A snuffbox?" The lovely redhead wrinkled her nose at this latest object she'd taken from the sack. "That should have gone in Squint's bag."

While his tunic was coming down over his head, Palma said, "I'm as dedicated to my career as you are, you see, Angel. You're a skilled highway robber and I'm an ace photographer. Thus I must—"

Blam! Wham!

"By St. Charlie's bones! What is that?" The Scarlet Angel ran to the open window. "Palma, my beloved, it's Laranja West troops. They're retreating through the woods."

"Maybe they'll retreat right on by," he said and he got all his cameras around his neck.

"Nay, I fear not. I see their sergeant motioning at

this very inn," the girl said. "Come, we must get out of here at once."

"Wait till I pull my pants on. I recently made a vow never to leave anyplace untrousered." When he was dressed, he joined her at the window. "Dozens of them, all pouring into our courtyard."

Down below, beyond the edge of the thatch roof, men in dirty and tattered red and white uniforms were stumbling and staggering into the flagstone court of the Knuckle & Chin.

Thump! Whack!

"There goes the front door," said the Scarlet Angel. "I very much fear any way of exit is now—"

"Nope, we can get out. See, we just jump onto the roof out there and then to the stable roof." He pointed. "With luck we can get a couple of mounts and get out the back way without being spotted."

"Aye, I do believe we can, admirable Palma mine."

He dived across the room and grabbed up the pouch of gold coins. "We'll need traveling expenses."

"You remain very calm under pressure."

"I've gone out of a lot of bedroom windows." Eyes narrowed, he watched the courtyard. "Most of them are inside, down in the dining room by now. Let's be up and doing." He stepped over the sill and waited for the Scarlet Angel to join him.

They made their way silently down the slightly slanting roof. Just as they reached the edge and Palma was about to leap to the stable roof four feet away a straggling Laranja West soldier chanced to look up.

His mouth opened, and his gun hand swung for his

holster. Then he stiffened and toppled over against a water barrel.

"Jump," urged the redhead, holstering her stungun.

"Much obliged." He leaped.

The Scarlet Angel followed.

Palma scurried across the wooden stable roof on hands and knees, then swung down through a window hole. "Still pretty agile for somebody who spends so much time in bed." He landed on the straw, then saw to it that the horses all remained calm by patting and cajoling them.

They'd finished saddling two horses when a great howling began in the woods.

"Kill! Kill!"

"Death! Death!"

"Murder! Murder!"

"More visitors." Palma hurried to the shut door at the front of the stable and took a cautious glance through the narrow opening.

Troops in blue and gold uniforms were pouring forth out of the surrounding forest. They waved knives, pistols, and clubs, screaming and howling. Their eyes were wide, and the hair of many of them stood on end.

"Death! Death!"

"Murder! Murder!"

"Laranja East troops this time," said Palma. "A zealous lot, too."

The Laranja West soldiers in the inn began firing out at the howling troops who came charging at them. Twenty of the East troops went down, dead. More rushed out of the woods, screaming, frenzied.

"Let's be off." Palma led his horse to the rear of the

stable and carefully pushed the door open. The narrow trail away from here was as yet empty of soldiers of either side.

He and the Scarlet Angel rode swiftly away from the Knuckle & Chin.

After they'd covered several miles, the girl said, "There is, I sense, something you wanted to tell me, cherished Palma. What is it?"

"Oh," he replied, "I was going to suggest we leave the inn."

CHAPTER 13

———◆———

Toot!

"Excuse me," said the steam robot. "My boiler has been defective ... *toot* ... for no little time and consequently ... *toot* ... due to other flaws in my structure the escaping steam often produces a most unseemly ... *toot* ... toot sound. Pray excuse me."

Summer had just been introduced to Thinker, the meal-serving mechanism. "Think nothing of it," he said. "What I'd like to—"

"What's for dinner tonight?" inquired Hesslin, putting his whiskers close to the steaming caldron Thinker had wheeled in.

"It's ... *toot* ... boiled offal," replied the steam robot.

"Again?" Young Hare groaned. "I take it the management of this alleged asylum took no notice of the nine-page critique of the bill of fare which I—"

"What's that blue stuff floating there in the offal?"

Thinker's neck creaked as he bent to gaze into the caldron. "Appears to be part of somebody's felt hat, doesn't it?"

"Isn't it bad enough they feed us offal practically every day?" demanded the catman. "Does it have to be contaminated as well?"

"Ah, but, Mr. Hesslin . . . *toot* . . . under the amended Territorial Pure Food and Drug Statutes offal may contain as much as ten percent non-offal." Thinker snapped his metal fingers, which made a *thung* sound. "Drat, I meant to toss in that dead mouse I found on the floor of Dr. Ferrier's—"

"*Cats* like mice," Hesslin said slowly. "Cat*men* do not like mice. For an intelligent machine you—"

"Excuse me . . . *toot* . . . for being confused," said the robot. "Since the philosophical anarchist dog-faced boy on subfloor B is always asking for bones I naturally—"

"I'm not some kind of sport of nature."

"Boys, boys," said Dr. Yach. "Enough quarreling. Go ahead, Thinker, and pass out the offal."

"Yes, I . . . *toot* . . . will. Don't you have a bowl, Mr. Summer?"

"That's OK. I'm fasting," said the reporter. "You go to Dr. Ferrier's cell every day?"

While Thinker spooned the hot food into the other inmates' wooden bowls he said, "Three times a day. Lately I've been . . . *toot* . . . dropping in more often to . . . *toot* . . . get rid of the dead mice."

"Damn," said Hesslin. "Talk of something else while I'm eating my offal."

"*Toot* . . . excuse me."

"Do you know why Dr. Ferrier is being kept in St. Charlie's?" Summer asked the robot.

"It has to do . . . *toot* . . . with some contribution . . . *toot*—"

"Lord almighty!" Bright-haired Hare threw his unfinished bowl of offal against the wall. "Can't you control that offensive tooting of yours?"

"Now, now," said Dr. Yach, "we can't all have complete sway over ourselves, young fellow ... God bless the king!"

"Oh, screw the king!"

The robot wiped his spoon on his bibbed apron. "I will now ... *toot* ... wish you a hearty ... *toot* ... good evening."

Summer caught his arm. It was blazing hot and he quickly let go. "Wait, Thinker. You were telling me about Dr. Ferrier, the reason he's here."

Thinker walked to the cell door. "He made a great contribution to ... *toot* ... the war effort."

"Why lock him up for that?"

"I must run." The door was opened from the outside, and Thinker and his caldron clattered away.

When the door was shut Summer said, "He's got a defective boiler."

"We all have our little flaws." Dr. Yach licked his fingers, then pushed his empty bowl aside. "As one grows older—"

"He's overheating," said Summer. "So it's possible he may explode."

"I would hate to think so," said the bearded old man. "Thinker and I have been through a good deal over the years. I'm certain he always saves the best offal for this cell."

The catman wiped his whiskers clean. "Are you suggesting, Summer, that it might be possible to cause Thinker to explode at a specific time?"

"Yeah, I am. To explode when he's standing right next to this door. He doesn't even have tinker-proof gauges, so it should be fairly simple to—"

"Never, sir, never." Dr. Yach grunted to his feet. "That robot is like a member of the family."

Hesslin stroked his chin fur. "There are six other doors between us and the ground level, though, Summer. Supposing we could blow our way out of this cell, we'd still have—"

"I'm not saying we're going to do it the next time Thinker comes in. There's a lot more about the layout of St. Charlie's I want to know first."

"Monstrous. To plot the cold-blooded murder of a loving, loyal machine simply to further—"

"He might not be the only one who goes," Hesslin warned the old doctor. "I don't want to rot here, or turn into a quivering wreck like you. If you try to foul up any escape plan I swear I'll—"

"I don't quiver."

"The whole thing sounds foolhardy," put in Hare, "and yet—"

Thump! Thump!

Dr. Yach blinked. "Who can that be thumping on our cell door at this hour? We never have callers after dinner, never. Can they have received word already of your monstrous designs on—"

"Shut up!" said the catman, hunching and watching the door.

"Special charitable visitor," announced a thin voice outside.

It's the princess, Summer told himself.

The heavy door opened. "What a wonderful feeling, to be able to do something worthwhile with my vast fortune."

A plump birdman stepped in. It was Mulligan, the Starbuck claimant.

CHAPTER 14

Rain hit the ironwork and glass hard and fast, then rolled more slowly down the curving sides of the huge domed buildings. The night wind shook the wild grass and tangles of spiky weeds that filled the wide streets.

"It was lovely here once," said the Scarlet Angel, the wind worrying her long red hair. "I remember being brought one autumn when I couldn't have been more than ten. Very gawky I was then.

They were leading their horses along an overgrown street which cut through the center of the long-abandoned exposition grounds.

"You could never have been awkward, Angel."

"Ah, but I was. Long and lean, skinny and hardly more sure on my feet than a newborn colt."

In the center of the weedy street loomed a fifty-foot-high statue of a military gentleman who held a sword on high. Since the statue had been made not of metal or of stone but of some kind of papier-mâché the old campaigner had several gaps in him where his mesh-wire skeleton showed through. His sword was in a particularly woeful shape.

"I truly appreciate your helping me out," said Palma.

"Since it was my fault you missed your rendezvous in Ravenshoe," said the girl, "it is only fitting that I arranged another meeting with Tully Keep."

"Little did I realize you and the celebrated guerrilla were chums."

"Outcasts of various kinds tend to get acquainted." She nodded to their right, turned onto a weed-thick lane leading by a vast grass-infested trough which had once been a marble pool. The fountain rising up from the pool's center was made of the same material as the giant soldier.

"I expected to find guerrillas camped out in the mountains or the jungle."

"The Crystal Gardens lie at the edge of an area that's seen much fighting in recent years. No one has visited it in a good long while, so it makes a suitable temporary headquarters for Tully Keep and some of his men," said the Scarlet Angel. "Obviously he never stays in one place long."

"Keep's not on either side really, is he?"

"He believes King Waldo and the government of Laranja East are corrupt and must be replaced. But the rulers of Laranja West are hardly better," explained the girl. "He, therefore, opposes both sides. It's his hope that he'll be able to bring off a coup and—"

"Oops!" Palma noticed a man, inside a glass-walled exposition building, watching them. The man wore a two-piece woodsman suit and held a blaster rifle. "A guard over there."

"Yes, he's the third we've passed since we passed through the gates."

"My keen eye is losing some of its keenness. This is the first guy I've spotted."

At the end of the lane was a circular building of multicolored glass panels and white wrought iron. In the doorway, arms folded, stood a white-furred cat-man. He smiled, making a purring sound, and came out into the hard rain. "Angel," he said as he embraced the girl, "still a road agent, eh, dear friend? When are you going to abandon those defective oafs and come over with us?"

Three men appeared from out of the wet darkness. They led the horses away.

"Your profession simply doesn't pay as well as highway robbery, Tully." The girl backed out of his arms. "This is Palma, one of the most excellent photographers in the Barnum System or the entire—"

"I know your work, my friend." The guerrilla leader held out a paw. "You've done some splendid picture spreads for *Galactic Geographic.*"

"Yes, I have," agreed Palma.

"You want to talk to me, my friend?" Keep beckoned them to follow him into the multicolored dome.

There were even rows of flower beds crisscrossing the circular gravel floor, the flowers long since dead or taken over by magnificent weeds.

The white-furred catman led them to the center of the large room and offered them white wrought-iron chairs.

Palma sat close to the Scarlet Angel, resting one hand on her shoulder. "I had some questions to ask you when I commenced on this quest, Keep," he said. "En route a few more things have aroused my curiosity."

"You want to know if good King Waldo is the Phantom of the Fog," said Keep. "We'll come to that topic in a moment ... but what are your more recent sources of puzzlement, my friend?"

"We had our path crossed at the Knuckle and Chin," continued the bald photographer. "The Laranja West troops behaved pretty much like soldiers I've encountered in most parts of the universe. The Laranja East lads, though, didn't. They appeared to be crazed, considerably goofy. Reminded me of some Venusian Buddhists I met once who had the habit of now and again running amok."

Keep nodded. "So they're field-testing it on a much larger scale than we figured at first."

"Testing what, Tully?" asked the red-haired girl.

"You must know something, Palma, about the use of chemical and biological weapons."

"Sure, people have even used them on me," he answered. "All that kind of thing was outlawed by the Barnum Accords of a few years back. No planet, no territory in our system is supposed to use anything like that."

"This particular chemical-biological invention is being used by Laranja East on its own troops," said the catman.

"Something to pep them up?"

"Exactly. It's a spray. One whiff and your average soldier turns, for a period of an hour or more, into a kill-crazy and absolutely fearless warrior."

Thoughtfully Palma rubbed at the rain-speckled top of his head. "Any idea who invented the stuff?"

"The spray is being manufactured, at a secret factory somewhere in Laranja East, by the Starbuck clan."

"How about a guy name of Dr. Ferrier ... is he connected with the Starbucks?"

Keep said, "Not that we know. Why?"

"His name came up." Palma twisted a strand of the Scarlet Angel's hair around a finger. "You have an inside source of information about the activities of the Starbuck folks."

Keep grinned, whiskers perking. "Yes, my friend, a fairly highly placed informant."

"Aha! The claimant is a fake—he's one of yours."

"Yes, the Mulligan Starbuck you met at the family estate is working for us," said Keep. "When we first got wind of this new killer-producing spray some months ago I decided we needed a better source of Starbuck facts than we had."

The rain bounced on the colored panels high above. Palma watched that for a moment. "Mayhew, our stringer—he was supplying information to you, too, wasn't he?"

"Yes. I'm sorry they did him in."

"That was to keep him from telling Summer and me anything. Mayhew was able to mention two people before he died: you and this Dr. Ferrier."

"Mayhew never lived to pass on what he knew about Ferrior to me," said the guerrilla.

"Could be Ferrior is the chap who invented the stuff," said Palma. "And it is possible the king is sniffing the spray himself on the sly."

"That would explain why he turns into a nighttime killer ... yes," said Keep. "If Mayhew believed that, I tend to believe it as well. What we lack, as yet, is proof."

"Mayhap by now Summer's got something out of Ferrier," Palma said. "Oh, yeah, another thing I'm curious about."

The Scarlet Angel said, "The stagecoach."

"Yep, the coach. Right after I left it the damn thing exploded," said the photographer. "Due to the fact I was being dragged off into the wilds by a gang of cutthroats I didn't get a chance to go back and dig into the wreckage. I know some kind of bomb had been planted."

"We didn't plant it, if that's what you're thinking," Keep told him. "We only use that sort of device on rare occasions, against important government toadies."

"You haven't heard any scuttlebutt about who arranged the fireworks?"

"None, friend Palma."

Palma said, "I have to assume the people who got rid of Mayhew were trying to do me a similar favor. Which means all my cautious skulking around in the wilds of Laranja East hasn't been as unobtrusive as I hoped."

"You were not followed here to the Crystal Gardens, that I can assure you. You and Angel are free to remain here for—"

"Nope. I'm about due to meet my partner back in the capital."

The Scarlet Angel said, "We are to part then, dear Palma?"

"Not until tomorrow," he said.

CHAPTER 15

—————◆—————

"You can eat the apples, the zingos, the grout sand-wiches, and the saltwater taffy," said Mulligan Star-buck while lifting the checkered cloth off the picnic basket hanging over his feathered arm. "Don't, how-ever, touch the gherkins, the pemican-on-rye sand-wiches, the popcorn balls, or the tomato. Oh, and you can drink the lemonade but not the iced tea."

"What sort of benevolent visit is this?" complained Hesslin. "I haven't had a gherkin since I was locked away to rot and now you—"

"The reasons for the restrictions will soon make themselves manifest." Mulligan set the wicker basket on the cell floor and motioned Summer to follow him into a corner. Moving was easier for the reporter now, though still painful. "I'm breaking my cover sooner than I'd intended, Summer. After Princess Joline told me you were here I decided you'd have to be sprung. If all goes well we'll get Dr. Ferrier, too. Won't be a bad night's work." He stroked his beak. "I'm not who you thought."

"You mean those are fake feathers?"

"Oh, I'm an authentic birdman, but I'm not the Starbuck heir," he explained. "I'm an agent for Tully Keep."

"My partner's been looking him up. How does the princess fit in?"

"Joline isn't quite as dim-witted as she likes to appear. She, unbeknown to her father, has been aiding various liberal causes for quite some time. She has also, now and again, provided us with information. Joline is aware that I'm a false claimant. When she determined you were really Jack Summer she paid me a visit at the estate. The result of which you see."

"I figured she'd forgotten all about me."

"A common feeling when you're locked up, as I well—"

"Gah, these are the toughest gherkins I've ever sunk a—"

"I cautioned you against them." Mulligan snatched the green pickle from Hesslin's paw.

Old Dr. Yach was slowly chewing on a chunk of taffy. "Perhaps you can explain the real purpose of your visit."

"I'm here to help the lot of you escape from St. Charlie's," replied Mulligan.

"Escape from here is well-nigh impossible," said Hare.

"Not if you apply technology and money," said Mulligan. "Thanks to Lady Thorkin's fondness for me I've been able to avail myself of both." He dropped to his knees beside the yellow basket. Resting the pickle on his palm that Hesslin had tried to nibble, he opened it down the center to reveal a squat silver rod. "Universal lockpick."

Hare asked, "Don't they have some sort of detection gear visitors have to submit to?"

"This thing's made out of a new Starbuck alloy the

average friskmachine (also made by the Starbucks) cannot detect," explained the birdman. "My only problem in swiping this lockpick from one of the family labs was picking the lock to get at it."

Hesslin stopped eating, reached out and took up the lockpick. "After we use this on our door, then what?"

"The iced tea." Mulligan unscrewed the cap on the thermos. Unseaming his tunic he poked at his chest feathers. "Which one ... ah, yes, here." He plucked a feather and dropped it into the liquid in the thermos. From the picnic basket he next took the tomato. "Made of a new Starbuck plastic. Stuff it into the top of the jug, like so, and it makes a spray nozzle. There we are. This particular spray will knock out any guard as far away as five feet."

Dr. Yach said, "My optimism is growing. We may finally get out of St. Charlie's."

Mulligan gathered up the three popcorn balls. "Miniaturized stunguns. Here's the barrel ... you have to pull it out through the stickum. Aim the ball, squeeze it, and your opponent freezes." He stood. "Now I'll outline the escape plan, and the route we'll be taking. We have to spring Dr. Ferrier, too."

Hare was staring down at the picnic basket, mouth downturned. "What about the pemican-on-rye sandwiches? You told us not to touch them either."

"Oh, yes, I'm glad you reminded me." The birdman claimant took one of the sandwiches. "The sandwiches are for me. So busy putting this little show together I completely missed lunch and dinner."

"What's the use of escaping?" asked Hesslin as he finished his apple. "They'll only catch us again."

"No they won't," Mulligan promised. "I've arranged things so as to avoid that possibility. You, Dr. Yach, and young Hare will be smuggled into a neutral territory by an associate of mine who'll meet us outside the walls of St. Charlie's. I have a hunch you'll be able to return to Laranja East quite soon." He crossed to Summer. "You and I and Dr. Ferrier will remain in the capital, making our way to a hideaway I know of. You're up to traveling?"

"I'll make it; don't worry," Summer told him. "Let's go over the plan."

"I'm going to miss this old place," sighed Dr. Yach.

The universal lockpick worked perfectly. The knockout gas, sprayed through the judas hole by Dr. Yach, had put their most immediate guard, the one who'd escorted Mulligan, quietly to sleep.

"So this is the corridor," whispered Dr. Yach as he rotated his head to take in the dirty walls and the water-stained ceiling. "I was unconscious when they locked me away eighteen years ago, thus I don't believe—"

"That's enough nostalgia," said Hesslin, who held a popcorn-ball stungun in his right paw. "We have to extricate Dr. Ferrier and then get the hell out of St. Charlie's."

With Mulligan leading they eased along the long, curving corridor.

"Guard!" Hare saw him first, and squeezed his stungun.

The big lizardman stiffened, one foot in the air, in the act of coming around a corner.

They continued on.

"This is Ferrier's cell." Mulligan's feathered hand touched the lockpick to the heavy door.

The door creaked open.

"Don't interrupt me, don't come intruding in on me," said Dr. Ferrier. He was hunched on the cell floor, his back to them. "Dead in under ten seconds, under ten seconds. We're moving right along."

"Hey, Dr. Ferrier." Summer stepped across the threshold.

The catman didn't turn around. "I've already had my night's offal. I'll thank you to leave me alone, leave me in peace." Using its tail as a handle he picked up the mouse he'd just succeeded in killing. "An amazing breakthrough, using only ingredients scraped from the cell walls plus—"

"We've come to get you out of this goddamned place," said Summer as he took hold of the doctor's shoulder.

The scientist looked at him. "This is some sort of escape attempt, an attempt at escape, is that what you mean?"

"Yeah, and it's been going pretty good up until this point," said Summer. "You can bring your mouse or leave it, but let's move."

"Cat*men* don't eat mice," said Hesslin from the doorway. "*Cats* eat mice. There's no need for slurs at a—"

"Dr. Ferrier, please, come along," urged Mulligan. "We're operating on a fairly tight schedule."

"On a tight schedule, a tight schedule is it? Well, very well." Dropping the dead mouse and rising, he accompanied Summer out of the cell.

"Guard!" came the warning whisper of Dr. Yach.

"I'll use this knockout gas on him. Now where's that trigger again?"

"What in the perishing bloody hell do you ruddy blooming loonies think you're—"

"Ah, I remember. This is how it works." The bearded old man succeeded in spraying the knockout mist directly into his own face. He toppled over.

"Of all the blasted blooming bloody idiot things I've—"

"There!" Hesslin froze the guard with his stungun.

Hare was beside the old doctor, poking him. "Wake up, Dr. Yach. We're escaping, remember?"

"He'll be out for hours," said Mulligan.

"Stand aside." Hesslin caught hold of the back of the slumbering doctor's tunic and lifted him onto his shoulder. "Now can we get on with this damn escape before we all rot here in the corridor?"

CHAPTER 16

———◆———

The wet wind grabbed the inn sign, ripped it from its hooks and sent it spinning through the night to skim Palma's rain-swept head. "The Nose and Foot Inn," he read as the sign passed over. "Another place commemorating a human tragedy, no doubt."

"Try not to say anything about Pegleg's not having a real nose," suggested the Scarlet Angel. "He's a mite self-conscious."

"Why do they call him Pegleg if he's missing a nose?" Palma dismounted and guided his horse into the low musty stable at the back of the inn.

"He lost a leg, too, in another war." She led her mount into one of the many empty stalls. "He used to operate an inn near Ravenshoe named the Leg and Beartrap."

"Sounds cozier than this place."

The girl, lips moist with night rain, kissed him. " 'Tis not the most auspicious place to spend our last night together, dear Palma," she said finally. "Pegleg, however, is one of the few innkeepers in this area who can be trusted."

"He knows who you are?"

"Yes, but he's not the kind who'd betray me," the

Scarlet Angel assured him. "Remember, don't say anything about his poor tin nose, or its being lopsided."

"I'll compliment him on his ears or chin, giving the impression I haven't noticed the nose at all."

"We could have stayed at the Crystal Gardens. Tully has several spare exhibition halls."

"All with an abundance of glass walls," he said. "This way, we also got twenty miles closer to the capital before stop—"

"Clutch the firmament!" ordered a tenor voice.

"Beg pardon?" Palma turned to face the man in the stable doorway.

The man waved his blaster pistol. "I mean, raise your mitts. Else I'll have no choice but to—"

"Pegleg, it's me," announced the Scarlet Angel, arms spread wide.

The innkeeper slowly lowered his gun. "I thought it was horse thieves. In fact, I'm still not at all certain your companion may not be a nagnapper."

"He's a dear friend, Pegleg. We'd like a room for the night."

Pegleg slipped his gun away under his apron. After a few seconds he began chuckling, rubbing his hands together. "Well, this is indeed fateful, Angel," he said. "You can help me celebrate."

"Surely. What are you celebrating?"

"My new nose." Pegleg tapped it fondly. "Is it not a beauty?"

"I can't see very well in this light."

"Why, of course you can't. What sort of innkeeper am I, not to invite the both of you inside on a foul night such as this? Come inside, do."

There was a substantial fire in the large stone fireplace of the dining room Pegleg led them to. "I was commencing to think the inclement weather would keep all customers away, thus affording me no opportunity to show off my new nose. Now then, What do you think of it, Angel?" The nose was of highly polished aluminum, reflecting the flames that flickered in the fireplace.

"A great improvement," she told him.

Pegleg took a step in Palma's direction. "I'd value your opinion of it, sir. What say you?"

Palma said, "I'm not allowed to discuss your nose."

"Eh?"

Shaking her head, the Scarlet Angel led Palma to the dinner table. "You needn't—"

"I like your ears, though," the bald photographer added as he tapped a few of his camera cases. "One sees so few matching ears, especially in my trade. A man with a symmetrical head is a rarity and should be complimented."

Pegleg tugged at one of his ears. "Why thank you, sir," he said. "Ah, by the by, Angel, take a gander at this." He rolled up the left leg of his pantaloons to display a gleaming new metal leg. The leg was of filigreed silver, encrusted with rubies and chunks of jade. "I've added this since last we met."

"Very handsome." The girl seated herself opposite Palma. "Obviously expensive."

"I won't bother to show you the toenails now, each is inset with—"

"Inherit some money, have you?" inquired Palma.

"No, nothing of the ... Ah, that is, yes. You've put your finger on it truly, sir." Pegleg lifted a menu off the mantle. "A dear great aunt of mine departed this life, leaving me a quite large and completely unexpected legacy."

"That's admirable," said Palma, "using the money to improve yourself."

The innkeeper inhaled with zest. "Breathing has taken on a whole new meaning since I had this nose installed. 'Twould bring a smile to your sweet lips, Angel, to see your old Pegleg sniffing rosebuds of a morning."

"Sniff them while you may," murmured Palma.

Pegleg presented him the menu. "The ox is very good tonight, should you be in the mood for ox."

"We'll need time to decide," the red-haired girl said.

"To be sure, dear, take all the time you wish." Pegleg backed toward the door. "I have a little something special in the wine cellar; 'twill add to the festivities."

As soon as the innkeeper was gone the Scarlet Angel asked, "What is it that's disturbing you, beloved Palma?"

"Where'd he get the money for the nose? Where'd he get the money for that leg?"

"No doubt he came by the money in some kind of shady deal," she answered. "Naturally enough, not knowing you, Pegleg doesn't want to discuss it openly. There's no need to—"

Clippety clop! Clippety clop!

Palma jumped up. "Usually the wine cellar is directly under the joint," he said. "He doesn't have to ride to it."

"Perhaps it is not ..." She ran to the window and drew aside the rough-spun curtains. The rain was slamming hard against the leaded panes. "I can't see the horseman at all."

"Best to sit yourself down, Miss Angel." A very tall and wide young catman had entered, a pistol in each paw.

"Jacques? Surely you do not aim those at me?"

Jacques's whiskers dropped. "We've had a change of policy, Miss Angel."

"Who paid for the nose?" Palma rested a hand on one of the camera cases that hung around his neck.

"Well," said Jacques, trying not to meet their eyes while yet keeping them covered, "the Territorial Police made the master an offer, which he accepted. If he but turn in those of his road-agent customers who chance to put up here at the Nose and Foot they will continue to provide him with much gold. He pondered long, you may be sure, Miss Angel, before he came to the conclusion . . . don't fool with those gadgets, sir."

"I was trying to decide which of my cameras to use to capture you on film, Jacques."

"Me? Why would you want a picture of me?"

"I'm on a roving assignment for Coult Publications." Palma's fingers unfastened the lid of the case. "We're especially eager to find interesting faces for *People, Etc.* Magazine."

Jacques gave a negative jerk of his furry head. "I wouldn't say I had an interesting face."

"You don't see yourself as I, with the eye of a trained artist, see you," said Palma. "True, it might perhaps make a more striking shot if you had perhaps an aluminum nose or . . ." He pulled a stungun from the case and shot the catman.

Before Jacques could squeeze the trigger of either of his blasters he stiffened.

"OK, let's make a hasty departure."

"I'm sorry I led you into a—"

"Apologize on the gallop, Angel." He stuck the stungun back in its case, then nodded toward a rear door of the dining room. "Can we get to the stable that way?"

"Yes." Dashing to the door, she yanked it open. "By way of the kitchen."

They ran along a wood-paneled corridor, across a steamy kitchen, and past a lizardwoman cook.

"Mercy me!" she exclaimed.

"They really do have an ox," observed Palma.

One more door and they were in the night and rain again.

The stable, a hundred yards away, they did not reach.

Three cloaked figures made that impossible. A cat-man, a green-feathered birdman, and a black man with a dead-white beard. All of them armed with shockrods and pistols.

"In the name of King Waldo and the sovereign territory of Laranja East," said the catman, the rain pelting him and making pocks in his fur, "I hereby charge you both with violating the laws and statutes forbidding robbery on the highway. I further charge you, miss, with being none other than the ruthless Scarlet Angel and you, sir, with being her paramour and accomplice."

"I am the Scarlet Angel." The girl stood straight, paying no attention to the hard-falling rain that was hitting at her. "This man, however, is an innocent traveler whose path happened to cross mine."

The lizard Territorial Policeman sneezed and laughed at the same time. " 'Tis hardly likely an innocent wayfarer would, purely by chance, come bounding out of the back door of the Nose and Foot with you."

"I'm Palma," explained Palma, "working for Coult Publications, out of the planet Barnum. You can contact their attorneys in—"

"You may once have been what you say, sir," said the catman. "This night, though, you are the companion of the Scarlet Angel. As such you will join her on the gallows. You will be hanged, drawn, and quartered. At the same time the Scarlet Angel is hanged."

"Well, if I'm going to die I'd like to snap a few last photos to send home to the folks." He reached for the camera case containing his stungun.

They were much quicker than Jacques. Two shocksticks hit Palma before he drew the weapon.

CHAPTER 17

———◆———

"We'll be safe in this part of the capital," said the spurious Mulligan Starbuck. With a feathered hand pressed to the slimy wall stones he was guiding Summer and Dr. Ferrier along the down-slanting alley. Thick gray fog was closer than the opposite wall.

"I don't believe ... I really don't believe I've ever been here in all my—"

"Slops!" A shuttered window snapped open up above, and a bucket of garbage was dumped out into the foggy night.

Summer dodged most of it. "Watch out."

Dr. Ferrier did not fare so well. "A most interesting, most interesting, style of life prevails here. What is this area called?"

"Suicide Slum." The birdman handed a real silk handkerchief to the doctor. "One of the things King Waldo vowed, on the eve of his coronation, was to clean up and beautify it."

"Slops!"

Splat!

"Not a drop, not one single drop, splashed me that time."

Summer aimed a question at the spot in the fog where he sensed the doctor was. "King Waldo didn't exactly keep his promises to you, did he, Dr. Ferrier?"

"No, he certainly behaved . . . Hum. I have the distinct impression I just stepped on a heap of animal dung. What could it have been?"

"Animal dung," said Mulligan.

"This is quite interesting, quite interesting," said Ferrier, "to see how the lower segment—"

"What made the king pop you into St. Charlie's?"

"That was because of Ferrier's Special Blend Number Three," answered the catman.

"What's—"

"Granny!"

Thud!

"That landed very hard," remarked Dr. Ferrier, glancing around at the encircling fog. "Must have been a good quantity, a very large quantity of garbage. And odd that they shouted 'Granny' rather than 'Slops.'"

"That's because it was somebody's grandmother," explained Mulligan. "They have a low opinion of old age in the slum."

Summer persisted as they progressed down the foggy alley. "What's Ferrier's Special Blend Number Three?"

"To more fully answer that, to answer it thoroughly, I'd best explain the nature of Ferrier's Special Blend Number One and, thereafter, Ferrier's Special Blend Number Two."

"You can do that later," Summer told him. "Tell me about Number Three, what it has to do with King Waldo and the Phantom of the Fog."

"I can fill you in," volunteered Mulligan. "Tried to give you some of what I found out when you visited the estate."

"We assumed you simply wanted to push your case for being the one and only authentic Mulligan Starbuck."

"Not at all, as you—"

"Estruma!" came a shout from above.

The doctor asked, "What's Estruma?"

Splat!

"Another word for slops."

"All over the front of me, the entire front of my garments. Most discouraging, very discouraging, when I was starting to believe I'd become most artful at dodging—"

"Slops!"

Splop!

"Again, yet again."

Mulligan took hold of Summer's arm. "You appear to be slowing down."

"Feel better than I did. Now tell me about this stuff."

"The special blend is a spray Ferrier concocted. He's been fooling with behavior-altering mists for years out at the university. Initially he was trying for stuff to control his students. You know, a squirt and they become attentive, insightful, possibly even a little more attentive. That was Number One. A few months ago he stumbled on Number Three. This spray was different."

"My greatest breakthrough, undoubtedly my greatest breakthrough to date," put in the doctor. "A perfectly useful, thoroughly useful, invention had it not been abused by our monarch."

They had reached the end of the alley. After groping at the fog for a moment, the birdman said, "This way next, to our left."

Up ahead, masked by the thick gray mist, there was a growling. Growling and snarling from several throats, snapping and yelping.

"A pack of animals lies in our path, directly in our path."

Mulligan slowed but did not stop. "Not animals, but they won't bother us," he said.

In single file they entered another alley. An old man lay flat on his back on the dirt, arms and legs widespread. Five boys, small and none older than seven, nearly naked, were tearing the old man's clothes from him as they searched for money and food. They snarled at each other, snapped and growled, while they worked.

"Not a good place to pass out," said Mulligan.

"This is indeed an education. I had no idea such things occurred in our city. My next spray will have to address itself to this problem. Yes, Ferrier's Special Number Four will—"

"You were explaining Number Three," Summer reminded the birdman.

"Number Three was for military use. You spray a whiff of Ferrier's Special Blend Number Three in the face of your average soldier—puff—he turns into a fighting dynamo, for an hour or so anyway."

"My intention was that the spray should be used to give courage to the soldier who might experience a moment of fear prior to battle. Little did I realize, had I but known, the military establishment would use it indiscriminately. No, such was not my original intention or, I need hardly say, I would never have donated Ferrier's Special Blend Number Three to the government of our territory."

"The stuff must have side effects, huh?" Summer asked. "That explains King Waldo."

"In some cases the blend is addictive," answered Mulligan. "Once you use it, you have to keep on."

"An effect, I might add, which had only turned up in point-oh-four percent of the laboratory tests."

"Why'd King Waldo start using the blend in the first place?"

"He's been worrying about getting old," said the claimant. "He figured the stuff would pep him up, since it'd boost a soldier's morale and stamina. Sometimes when you're sixty-one you get odd notions."

"It's happened before."

"Anyhow, the king started sniffing Number Three. He became a blend addict ... plus with him the stuff has an unusual side effect."

"It causes him to kill old ladies?"

"Yep, when King Waldo uses it he turns not into a fearless fighting man but a skulking strangler," said Mulligan. "I began to hear about that, pick up little bits of information, after I'd been inside the Starbuck mansion only a few days."

"We never had one strangler among our test subjects, not one, not a single—"

"Help! Bloody murder! It's him!"

From a street beyond the alley came a scream.

"The Phantom! It's the Phantom!"

Summer ran ... as best he could. The fog hid everything from him. Pointing himself at the screaming he yelled, "We're coming." He felt, rather than saw, that he was out of the alley. "Where are you?"

Only silence now. The fog was hanging motionless all around him.

Something over there. He could make it out through the fog. Black, a cloak. Summer headed for what he guessed must be the cloaked Phantom.

The Phantom was aware of him. He spun, leaving his victim half strangled. Hat pulled low, cloak wrapped around him, he ran into the fog.

Summer pursued him though he couldn't seem to cut down the distance between them. A pain was developing in his side.

The Phantom of the Fog dived into another alley.

Summer went after him.

"Slops!"

Splash!

Directly in Summer's path the garbage and dung fell. Both his feet hit it and he went sliding. He flapped his arms, hollered, but couldn't get his balance back. He banged into the tacky wooden wall on his left, and fell down flat in the mud and prior slops.

Though he made it to his feet again in under a minute, Summer knew the phantom was way and beyond catching.

"Summer?"

"Yeah, in here."

Mulligan materialized out of the mist. "The old woman is going to survive. Dr. Ferrier is helping her into the nearest flophouse. She's got no idea what the strangler looks like, says his face was all muffled," he said. "Are you OK?"

"For a guy who let the killer get away and then rolled around in shit, I guess I'm fine," said Summer.

CHAPTER 18

———◆———

"Quite a den of thieves, a veritable den of thieves," observed Dr. Ferrier from the top of the short flight of stone steps. "Where are we?"

"Den of Thieves number two-oh-six," said Mulligan, "one of the strongest, most active guilds on the whole planet."

"Who's your young friend, Mully?" inquired an enormous catwoman sitting at a wooden table near the entrance of the cellar. She raised a lopsided pair of black glasses off her eyes. "Looks like he's been rolling in cumshaw."

"We had an encounter with the Phantom," explained the claimant. "Almost laid hands on him, Blind Tabby."

"Almost."

The room was brick walled, its ceiling low. It was lighted by the score of candles on the tight-together tables. There were roughly fifty thieves and beggars here, almost all of them watching the newly arrived Mulligan, Dr. Ferrier, and Summer.

A man came rattling toward them, a glittering hand outthrust. "You must be Jack Summer, sir," he said. "I'm Sparkler, a great admirer of the incisive pieces you've penned. 'Tis my fond hope you'll have time to look into the dreadful way the Thieves and Cutpurses Relations Board is managed during your stay."

"I'd like to clean up first."

"Nobody minds a little dung around here." Pinned to the affable cyborg's chest was a paper sign announcing: *I am over 60% metal. Please help.*

Mulligan said, "Sparkler's the executive secretary of number two-oh-six. Also in sympathy with Tully Keep and our cause."

"Thieves won't fare any better than they do now," said Sparkler, "until we have a more enlightened form of government."

"What a feast for the eyes, a real feast for the eyes and the intellect." The catman was slowly taking in his candle-lit surroundings.

"Should you have some time, Jack Summer, I'd like to introduce you to some of the other chaps in the guild."

"Got nothing else to do at the moment but hide."

"Fine, then." Sparkler put his bright metal hand under Summer's arm and led him to a nearby table.

A plump man was sitting there eating cheese and black bread and then watching his insides. This was made easy by the plastic window set in his chest and stomach. "You can watch for nothing, Summer," he invited. "I'm Trollybag, the human physiological museum. See the innermost workings of the body, the romance of digestion, and many another wonder all for a single Joline. Cheap at twice the price."

"You must be the center of all eyes at dinner parties."

"I don't get invited out to dinner much."

"Trolly's our treasurer and over here's another of

our officers." Sparkler moved to a farther table. "Pick-purse Red, Jack Summer. Go easy, Red, he's nothing in his pockets, being fresh out of St. Charlie's."

"Yeah, so I just learned." The cardinal-headed bird-man nodded at Summer. "Pleased to meet you. In my own particular line I'm as gifted as you are in yours."

"An incisive pickpocket, huh?"

"I'm the cream of the crop, the top of the heap. If something's in a pocket, I can get it."

"You're no doubt growing anxious to remove that dung," said Sparkler. "I'll introduce you only to our sergeant-at-arms before allowing Mulligan to escort you to your private quarters. Here he is, the illustrious Dr. Roarer."

The extremely fat lizardman was dressed in a threadbare yellow suit, sitting alone at a table with a flower-patterned carpetbag beneath his folded green hands. "I'm extremely pleased to make your acquaintance, sir. I hasten to point out, lest there be some misunderstanding in the future, that I am not a doctor of medicine but rather a doctor of podiatry. Would you care to have me examine your feet? As a friend of dear Mulligan the fee will be nominal. Put your feet right up on the table . . . even one foot will do for a start. The foot, as you are no doubt aware, is at the heart of all physical ills."

"My feet are about the only part of me still functioning one hundred percent OK," said Summer.

"Perhaps you so believe, sir." Dr. Roarer dug a hand into the carpetbag, rattling the bottles and vials. "Don't be offended, however, if I point out that a man with feet operating at their peak does not fall down and appear before us all beshitten. I suggest, and bear in mind I do not prescribe but only advise, that you at least apply a spoonful of—"

"Come along," suggested Mulligan. "I'll show you to the room I've set aside for you."

Summer followed him across the low room and through a wooden door. The room they entered was small, with a wood-framed bed in one corner and an oil lamp burning on the small round bedside table. A ball-style TV set, looking newer than anything else, floated near the bed.

Seated, very stiff and straight, on the bed itself was Princess Joline. "Good evening, Mr. Summer. I'm very happy to see you got away with no trouble." She rose, holding out her hand.

"Do I genuflect and kiss it?" He moved no closer to the lovely blond.

"Perhaps you'd best leave us, Mulligan," the princess said.

"Sure thing, Princess. I have to get Ferrier settled in for the night." He left them.

There was a single chair in the room. Draped over it was a two-piece streetsuit.

"We assumed, rightly I see, that you'd need a change of clothes. The size is right, I think, based on information I found in one of those *Muckrake* bios of you."

"So you finally got around to reading them." Summer picked the suit off the chair back.

"You'd best keep in mind, Mr. Summer, that it takes time to arrange an escape from a place like St. Charlie's. We got you out as soon as we could."

"You going to watch me change, or are you going to get out?"

"I'll turn my head away. I have more to say to you."

Summer shrugged, tugged off his boots, and dropped his pants. "If it's an apology, you can skip it."

"No, I have no apology to make. I've already told you we all worked as fast as we could."

"Sure. I'm luckier than old Dr. Yach. Took eighteen years to bust him out."

"You must believe me, Mr. Summer, when I say I was not aware of all the uses St. Charlie's is being put to."

Summer pulled his tunic up over his head. "If my old man ran a loony bin I'd make it my business to find out what went on inside."

"Damn you, Summer, what do you . . . excuse me." Angry, she'd whirled around to point a finger at him.

Summer was standing there in his allseason underwear. He ignored the princess and got into the two-piece suit she'd brought. "Not a bad fit."

"You're going out of your way to be nasty to me."

"It's not out of my way, Princess."

Breathing rapidly, lips pressed tight, she walked up to him. "You're feeling sorry for yourself, that's why you're picking on me."

"Damn right I'm feeling sorry for myself, Princess. Thanks to your dad, good King Waldo, I spent several very long days in St. Charlie's and had a bunch of guys beat the crap out of me, pull out some of my fingernails, relocate most of my insides, and prod my private parts with an electric rod. Yeah, I'm sorry about the whole darn thing." He seamed the fly of the pants, seamed the tunic. "You go around fluttering your eyelashes and making your big green eyes go wide and bite that lower lip of yours and pretend you're an innocent lamb and everything is a big surprise to you. Maybe so. But I know it was on your father's orders I was stuck in St. Charlie's. That doesn't make me feel any too kindly toward his only daughter."

"My eyes aren't green, they're blue-gray."

"My perceptions aren't at their best right now."

"Are you well enough to go to bed?"

"Doesn't take much to go to bed. You just stretch out, pull up the covers, shut your—"

"I mean with me," amplified the princess.

Summer's eyebrows rose. "I hadn't thought about it."

"No? I thought all this feigned anger of yours was all part of the preliminaries, part of your courtship routine."

After a few seconds Summer smiled. "You know, you're probably right."

CHAPTER 19

———◆———

"Step lively, you scum," ordered the black man with the white beard as he prodded Palma in the kidney region with the dead end of his shockstick. "The RM is most anxious to have a bit of an interlude with you."

The three Territorial Policemen were urging Palma and the Scarlet Angel along a neolinoleum hallway in the capital city's Worst Offenders Prison. It was early morning, and they'd been traveling all night by coach and then freight train.

The bald photographer rubbed at his back with one hand and at his head with the other. "Considering we're such prize prisoners, you didn't transport us in a very high-class fashion. I'm fairly certain that freight car was previously used to haul—"

"Keep moving, you cutthroat rascal!" The black policeman prodded him once again.

"'Tis no use to attempt communicating with them, dear Palma," the Scarlet Angel said sadly.

"Save all your wise talk for the RM," advised the catman.

"Who's the RM?"

"You'll find that out soon enough, you gallows bird."

"Maybe I can persuade him to let me contact one of the Coult attorneys on—"

Pooml Kabloom!

"Sounds like he's in an especially foul mood this morning," said the green-feathered policeman.

Palma, "That was the RM who produced that sound?"

"Not half of what he can do when his boiler's on the blink."

Pooml Pooml Slam!

"Has a boiler, does he?"

"Right through that door marked Robot Magistrate, if you please."

Palma was fleet enough to avoid the prod this time. A small courtroom met him beyond the oaken door. Behind a high desk sat a gunmetal robot in judge's robe and wig. Steam was puffing out of his right ear and between several of the metal fingers which held the gavel.

A small round-shouldered catman stood before the judge, forlornly rubbing at a still bloody gash over his eye. "You can't be serious, RM?" he asked in a stunned voice.

Bloom! Bim!

The judge's wig flew a few inches off his head, shoved by a puff of steam. When it settled again the Robot Magistrate said, "I never jest. Fifty-six years on the lettuce farm for you, Lightfinger Neddy, and ten strokes of the whip each morn before breakfast. Next case."

"But, RM, I've a dreadful allergy to lettuce. Makes me fur—"

"Drag the wretch away."

The only other occupants of the room were two very large lizardmen in gold and white uniforms. They rushed forward, caught Lightfinger Neddy by the elbows, and rushed him away through a swinging door.

Flum! Spoom!

The wig went up nearly two feet, smoke spilled out of both the RM's ears, and his left eyeball popped out to go sailing over his high desk.

Palma caught the eyeball. "Allow me to return your orb, your honor."

"Sir, take your roguish hands off my eye!" boomed the Robot Magistrate. "Do you know the penalty for touching a judge's eye?"

"Not offhand. Does it involve the lettuce farm?" He still held the plastic eye.

"Return that at once, swine!"

"Here, catch."

The robot judge missed, the eye hit the wall behind him, bounced, and dropped again to the courtroom floor.

"You despicable cur!" bellowed the RM. "First you touch my eye, then you fling it about as though it were a baseball."

"I wouldn't throw a baseball like that. A baseball I'd throw overhand."

"Silence!" The robot was kneeling behind his desk, slapping his metal hands on the floor as he searched for his missing eye. "Aha! Here it is." He reappeared with both eyes in place, and commenced consulting the papers spread out on the desktop. "Ah, yes. So you, sir, are Palma, alias the Bald Assassin, alias the

Hairless Avenger. The notorious traveling companion of the ruthless Scarlet Angel."

"I'm Palma the photographer. If you'd allow me to contact the attorneys—"

Boom! Wam!

The robot rose up several feet off the bench, and landed with a clang. "Sir, a highwayman has no right to counsel, especially a baldheaded highwayman who makes a habit of fondling judges' eyes."

"Your honor," said the Scarlet Angel, "this gentleman is not what you say."

"Ah, you I presume are the infamous slut known as the Scarlet Angel, the highway robber who has cut a bloody swath across the roads and byways of this territory for lo! these many years."

"I am indeed the Scarlet Angel," replied the redhaired girl. "Palma, I can assure you, is merely a photographer who journeyed here from Barnum to do a story on highway robbery."

"No one ever wants to write about magistrates," muttered the robot.

"I'd snap your picture," said Palma, "if these lads hadn't confiscated all my equipment."

The Robot Magistrate hammered on the desk. "Enough of this useless jawing. Let us get on with the sentencing."

Palma asked, "What happened to the trial?"

The judge ignored him, picking up a sheet of foolscap and reading from it. "Scarlet Angel, I hereby sentence you, for crimes too numerous to mention, to be taken to the public gallows two days hence and thereon, at high noon, to be hanged and thereafter your vile body buried in potter's field. Palma, for similar crimes against the territory, I do now sentence you to be escorted to that selfsame public gallows and to witness the hanging of the titian-haired harlot who has been your companion in crime and evil. After that you will have your turn on the gibbet and to be hanged by the neck until dead. Your body will then be cut into four quarters and your guts spilled on the paving stones.... Hold on a sec...." He picked up an electric quill to scribble in additions to the sentence. "Then the top of your bald skull will be sawed open and the hangman will step on your brains with dirty boots. Then your ears and nose shall be sliced off to be thrown to the hungry dogs that are always in attendance at such occasions. That should teach you to play games with a respected jurist's eye."

"Everything after the hanging part I don't expect will hurt much," said Palma. "But, listen, Judge, I must insist you allow me to contact—"

"Take them to their separate cells," ordered the robot. "Let us have the next case. Ah, this rascal has stolen a seedmuffin from a bakery, has he?"

The Scarlet Angel managed to touch Palma's hand before they were separated.

Palma scrutinized the cell wall. "Why does it say fluffy home-style hotcakes with fresh creamery butter and real maple syrup, then?" he asked the ordering mechanism set in the wall below the row of food slots. An illuminated breakfast menu glowed next to the ten slots.

"Because we serve fluffy home-style hotcakes with fresh creamery butter and real maple syrup," replied the voice grid.

"OK, so I'm in this condemned cell and it says right here on the bottom of the menu, 'Your choice of last meals.'"

"But this, sir, isn't your last meal. It's your first meal. You're not due for extermination for two days."

"How about fresh-squeezed orange juice and home-style Danish pastry, then? Can I have that?"

"You can have the fresh-squeezed orange juice."

"How come no Danish?"

"Your dietician won't permit it."

"Dietician? I haven't seen any dietician."

"She saw you, though, sir. Through the one-way wall in the courtroom."

Palma asked, "What does she say I can have?"

"A man with your chunky build and obvious anxiety-prone temperament should really watch the old carbohydrates, says she."

"I'm not chunky. She ought to see me with my clothes off."

"Prunes," said the voice of the food-serving mechanism.

"What's that mean?"

"Prunes is what you can have for breakfast, or a six-ounce serving of stewed yings."

"I'm not familiar with yings. What are they?"

"Well, a ying is a small purple fruit, wrinkled and quite similar to—"

"Prunes," said Palma. "OK, I'll have prunes and orange juice."

"You'll feel much better for it, sir, says she. Even during one's last days among the living a sensible change in diet can do a great deal of good."

Palma eased closer to the wall. "Can you make a

phone call for me? Try to get through to Jack Summer at the—"

"Oh, we can't do anything like that. Food is our
business, sir. Prunes and fresh-squeezed orange juice
coming up."

When the dish of prunes and the glass of juice appeared in two of the wall slots Palma took them to
the white-painted metal table and sat in a white-
painted metal chair.

His white-painted cell door opened. "Mr. Palma,
Mr. Palma, good morning." A blue lizardman with a
briefcase stepped in.

Behind him came a dapper parrot-headed man. The
door banged shut. "A very good head you have on
your shoulders, Palma. I like that head, that head will
move. Bert?"

"One hundred thousand at least, Howie."

"Two hundred thousand is more like it, Bert."

The lizardman leaned to his left, studying Palma.
"Could be, Howie. Yes, it definitely could be."

"Lawyers usually carry briefcases," said Palma.
"Would you lads be lawyers?"

"You can trust us, Palma," the parrot-headed man
assured him. "No need for a lawyer to tell you we've
got the fairest contracts in all the Barnum System."

"He's a little chunky," observed Bert, "but he'll look
good on a horse."

"Yeah, they'll love him on a horse. What do you figure we can count on selling?"

"A hundred thousand?"

"Make it two."

Palma got up from his prunes. "What are we selling, gents?"

"Didn't you give him our card, Bert?"

"My error, Howie. Here, Mr. Palma."

The photographer took the card. "Criminal Exploitations, Ltd. What are you, crooks?"

Howie laughed, beak clacking. "Crooks, he thinks, Bert."

Bert laughed, tongue flapping. "He thinks we're crooks, Howie."

"Palma, we are creators," explained the parrotman. "We bring romance and fantasy into the humdrum lives of everyday people. We weave the joys and tensions of life into fabrics of entertainment, fashioning new myths and mysteries for this jaded age. At the same time we educate, bring a moral message into millions of lives of myriad—"

"What are you selling?"

Howie took a breath. "Do you mean to tell me you've never heard of Criminal Exploi? Fill him in, Bert."

Bert snapped open his briefcase. "Salt and pepper shakers . . . you'll no doubt recognize the Wilton Mangler, he's pepper, and one of his nubile victims, she's salt." After flicking a little salt into his hand, he set the shakers next to the prunes. "Deck of cards . . . look, the Notorious Monster of Kirkham Street is the King of Hearts, his helpless victims make up the Queens and Jacks. Sold two hundred thousand. And here's a really nice one, sold over four hundred thousand. A board game entitled *Rape in the Fog*, the only fully authorized board game based on the vicious life and crimes of Iron Skull McNulty."

"We can't stress that *authorized* too much, Palma. It means your next of kin will receive a substantial royalty so long as any of the merchandise based on you and your vicious crimes stays in circulation. That can mean, at our generous four percent royalty, a tidy sum."

"For instance, the widow of the Butcher's Alley Fiend is still receiving checks," said the lizardman, "nearly seven years after his vicious dismemberments shocked the planet."

"Show him the book, Bert."

"Ah, yes, being a literary man yourself, Mr. Palma, you'll of course want to give us the right to produce a book based on your grim career as a knight of the road. This is a dummy our art and copy people whipped up this morning soon as we learned of your capture."

Palma took the book gingerly between thumb and forefinger. "*A Narrative of the Remarkable Life of the Notorious Palma, Giving an Exact Description of His Robberies, Escapes, etc. and Based on Previously Unknown Facts.* I have to admit I like the title; it has a bestseller ring to it."

"Will sell two hundred thousand in hardcover, one million in paper," said Howie. "Especially if we get all the juicy details of your romances into it."

"Might even make a series," said Palma. "The only real stumbling block I can see, gents, is this. I am not a highwayman. I'm a photographer, working for Coult Publications. Surely you've heard of us."

"Everybody's heard of Coult."

"Then instead of cluttering up my cell with all these trinkets, will you put through a call to somebody at Coult on Barnum ... ask for Fred Flowers. Tell him I need an attorney and fast."

Bert started gathering up the merchandise. "You're only one of the many convicted killers we deal with, Mr. Palma."

"If we make a fuss about you," amplified Howie, "we might well screw up our relationship with the whole of officialdom. We merchandise more than twenty killers, fiends, and monsters a year."

"You might as well sign with us," the lizardman said. "There are a number of competitors in this business, none of whom bother with getting permissions and authorizations. As you ride to the gallows you're going to see Palma toys, Palma games, and Palma books being hawked. Wouldn't it be a comfort to know your loved ones were going to turn a buck on some of that stuff?"

"OK, if you won't call Barnum," said Palma, "how about phoning my partner right here in Laranja East? His name is Jack Summer, he should be at the Laranja-Sheraton. Tell him—"

"Is that Jack Summer, the muckraking reporter?" asked Howie.

"The fellow who writes those incisive exposés from all over the universe?"

"That's the very Jack Summer I mean, yes. Call him for me."

The parrotman looked at the lizardman. "I've always been a fan of Summer's, Bert."

"As have I, Howie."

"Here's a chance to do him a possible favor. What say?"

"Risky."

"Nobody will know you called," Palma told them.

"We'll have to think it over, Palma."

"Sorry we can't do business," said Bert. "That head of yours would look great on a salt shaker."

CHAPTER 20

———◆———

"... Furthermore, asserted the Secretary of Famine, the reports of widespread hunger in areas over which fighting has been raging are highly exaggerated. Secretary Zwack pointed out that while a starvation death rate of twenty percent of the population of those areas might look higher, at first glance, than last month's figure of ten percent, it is not. Radicals and quislings have clouded the issue, averred the Secretary of Famine at this morning's press conference which followed a breakfast in the Lotus Room of the Laranja-Sheraton. Meanwhile our beloved monarch, King Waldo the second, has again broken in on all media to deliver another of his much-appreciated fireside talks. Here is a replay of the significant portion of that talk. . . ."

Directly in front of his eyes Summer saw smooth bare buttocks. Raising himself on an elbow he looked over the naked girl and saw the TV-ball floating close beside the bed.

A swarthy man, wearing a crown a size too large, was on the oval screen. "My fellow subjects, let me once again tell you that I am no killer. Such a thing would be pretty silly, wouldn't it? I mean, to be a king and a killer at the same time. You and I realize such a notion is silly, but certain radicals and quislings who continue—"

"Did I awaken you, Jack?" The unclothed princess placed a hand against his ear, reaching over her bare backside to do it. "I believe it's my duty to keep informed, so one of the things I unfailingly do is watch the midday news."

"It's midday already?"

"A few minutes beyond," Joline said.

". . . A man might be, say, a shoemaker and a killer or a dentist and a killer. There have been such cases. But, my fellow subjects, it's ridiculous to think a man would want to be a king and a killer. Let me tell you just being your king is plenty enough for me. I've always wanted to be king. Why, even when I was a little prince I—"

"I usually don't sleep till midday." Summer worked himself to the head of the bed and sat up.

"You usually don't spend the night with a princess after having been tortured for several days."

"True, that's true."

She looked at him again, away from the floating image of her father. "Were my life not dedicated to helping the people, Jack, it would be enjoyable to spend much time with you."

"You're right, though; our careers come first." He placed his hand on her back.

"The next few days, the next weeks will be very difficult," Princess Joline said. "I cannot, knowing what I now do, allow Father to continue on the throne. I've suspected his addiction to the war spray, and now Dr. Ferrier has confirmed it. To think that

Father could throw a man like Dr. Ferrier into St. Charlie's unjustly!"

"Or a man like me even." Summer slid his hand around until it rested just below her right breast.

"Yes, that's dreadful, too. The whole idea of what St. Charlie's has become is repugnant to me. To use a place meant for healing as nothing more than a political prison. I suspected something of this, but was trying not to see how corrupt and awful my father's reign has become."

Summer rubbed his forefinger over the breast's nipple.

". . . The message is plain, fellow subjects, I'm no killer. No, sir. Not me."

"Thus our beloved King Waldo the second once again stated he is not the Phantom of the Fog. Here in the studio with me is the noted political analyst, Sri Nogo. Sri, how did the king's protestations strike you?"

"Oscar, there's no doubt in my—"

"I'm Lanny."

"Yes, of course, Lanny. You're doing your fur like Oscar. Forgive me. There's no doubt in my mind, Lanny, that we've seen a man speaking the honest truth. I know what the radicals and the quislings are saying about the king . . . that he's lying in his teeth, that he's a base, grubby, weasel-pussed liar, that he's an ill-shaven, mealymouthed, dirty-linen swine, that he's a low-down, dirty, no good, rotten son of a bitch. Well, these charges are, in my opinion at any rate, exaggerations. Looking at this man sitting there by the snug palace fireplace, I was struck very forcibly with obvious honesty."

"Much the same impression I got, Sri."

"Certainly, Oscar ... oops, Lanny. Your fur-do keeps throwing me. Lanny, I think we can put to rest the rumors and lies which have been circulating."

"Thank you, Sri."

"Thank you, Lanny ... oops I mean ... no, it is Lanny, isn't it?"

"Jack, I really ought to watch the rest of the news," the princess whispered in his ear while she clung tightly to him. "You don't realize the responsibilities which weigh me down."

Summer stroked her hair.

"Oh, Jack, would that I were not born to rule."

"You can abdicate for an hour or so."

"Yes . . . yes, I suppose so."

". . . To the crime front. One of the most sensational arrests in the recent history of apprehension was made last night by the determined Territorial Police. And so it was that the ruthless Scarlet Angel, queen of the highwaymen, was trapped as she lay in the arms of her vicious paramour. . . ."

"We can turn this off now," murmured Joline as she reached toward the floating set. Her fingers did not quite make it to the switch.

". . . Here we see him, cowering as he is brought into the Worst Offenders Prison to begin his inevitable trip to the gallows. Notice he has the typical dark look and bald head of many habitual crimin—"

The princess succeeded in turning the set off. "Now, then, Jack."

"Wait now." He climbed off the naked girl to flick the TV on again.

". . . Known far and wide, hither and yon, as the

Bald Assassin, his career as a highwayman has come to its inevitable end."

"Palma!" Summer recognized his partner on the screen.

Joline asked, "Who's Palma?"

"He's not a highwayman."

CHAPTER 21

———◆———

"Those disreputable boots are going to do permanent harm to your feet," said Dr. Roarer, pointing with his free green hand.

"They form part of my disguise." Summer, wearing purple-tinted spectacles, a straw-colored beard, and a two-piece dung-collector's suit, was being guided by the lizard podiatrist along a quirky lane.

It was afternoon, but little sunlight made its way down through the overhanging rooftops and lines of drying clothes. Coming toward them down the alley was a funeral procession, all on foot. Four black-clad birdmen carried a wide wooden coffin on their shoulders, and six assorted mourners followed in single file.

Dr. Roarer tipped his orange stovepipe hat. "My sympathies," he said. "I warned him about his feet, but he paid me no heed."

"Stand aside, you crusty mountebank," said the left front pallbearer.

"Ain't a he anyhow, it's our poor departed grandmother we're toting," said the right rear.

"Male or female, sir, the eternal verity applies—healthy feet mean a long life."

"Gram was ninety-six when she crossed over, and

she had a wooden leg," left front told him. "Now out of the way."

Summer pulled the doctor to the side of the lane. "I've got an appointment to keep."

"After carrying that load all the way to the Paupers' Memorial Cemetery," Dr. Roarer called after the receding procession, "your own feet will be in need of attention. Today's special is Dr. Roarer's Foot Nostrum at four bottles for a Waldo."

The mourners shuffled on.

"This is the intersection we want up ahead, isn't it?" Summer asked as he and the doctor neared the corner.

"Let me see." From out of his hat Dr. Roarer took a pair of glasses. Adjusting them on his green nose, he said, "Butcher's Lane and Pesthouse Place. Right you are."

Summer adjusted the sign hanging around his neck and took a position in front of the wall of a day-old offal shop. The dangling sign announced: *Stricken Blind in the Prime of Life!! It Could Happen to YOU!! Please Give from the Heart!!*

Dr. Roarer set his flowered carpetbag gently on the cracked pavement. "Might as well do a little real business while providing you with a bit of protective coloration," he said while extracting a bottle of blue liquid from the bag. "You there, sir, there's still time to save the other one."

The pegleg bargeman ignored him, and went staggering on down the lane.

"Ah, here's a likely mark," said Dr. Roarer. "Crawling along on his hands and knees, a sure sign of foot trouble."

The young man was wearing a recently shredded two-piece business suit. His face was scribbled with gashes, cuts, and bruises. "... Waylaid ..." he muttered. "... Fallen upon by footpads ..."

Summer ran over to him. "Are you from Kaminsky, Kaminsky and Warren?"

"Indeed I am, sir," the battered young man said with a groan. "I'm Josiah Ramoz ... my card ..." His hand went clean through the remains of his coat and out again. "They seem to have stolen my pocket."

Summer helped him over against the offal shop and propped him up. "Somebody jumped you, huh?"

"Seven of them," replied the young attorney, "a company of thugs and footpads, consisting of three birdmen, two—"

"How did you wend your way here, sir, by which route?" Dr. Roarer uncapped the bottle of elixir.

"Why, the shortest way to my rendezvous with Mr. Summer seemed to be by way of Footpad Alley and then straight down Thug Lane."

"Well, sir, there's your explanation for what's befallen you. Footpad Alley is infested with footpads, hence the name."

"I assumed the name was a quaint throwback to an—"

"Did Mulligan Starbuck fill you in on the situation?"

The lawyer managed to straighten up some. "He is not the actual Mulligan Starbuck," he said. "I wouldn't want to say he is. This imitation Starbuck heir did, however, explain most of the circumstances of the problem to me. Of course I will maintain in court, unless directly questioned on the matter, that a hunted fugitive such as he never snaked in to see me at all."

"It seemed to me he'd have a better chance of reaching you than I would," said Summer. "I remembered your office had handled some legal work for Coult."

"Yes, we have served the Coult organization on several occasions. I have taken the liberty . . . what are you doing?"

Dr. Roarer had poured some thick pinkish elixir onto his hand and was rubbing it on Ramoz's cuts. "This would work more effectively if applied directly to your feet, but it's also wonderful for cuts, scrapes, and over a hundred other household ills."

"I don't have a household ill. Seven footpads—"

"The case," cut in Summer. "Let's continue with that."

"I have taken the liberty of contacting the Coult organization on Barnum, and Mr. Coult himself has given us *carte blanche* as far as expenses. He asked, by the way, how the article was—"

"What can you do for me and Palma?"

"Let me first . . . What's in that syrup? My head stings."

"All natural ingredients. Here, peruse the label, which I myself—"

"The case," reiterated Summer.

"Let me see if I have all the elements correctly," said the lawyer. "You, Mr. Summer, are an escaped lunatic and your partner, Mr. Palma, is a condemned highwayman who is to be executed tomorrow at noon. Is that about it?"

"Basically, yeah."

"Possibly we can get you a hearing before the Royal Lunacy Commission," said young Ramoz. "You look to me to be relatively sane. Let me say, by the way, that I am sorry to find you blind."

"I'm not blind, this is a disguise." He located an unbruised stretch of the lawyer's arm and gripped it. "I'm not crazy at all. I was railroaded into St. Charlie's because—I'm digging into the king's career as a murderer of old ladies."

"Oh, I'm glad we can have this chance to talk before we go before the commission, Mr. Summer. Almost makes the beating and robbing worthwhile. See, you don't want to say what you just said to me before the—"

"It's true. You live full time on this goddamn planet, you must know how the political setup works."

"Yes, I've heard some of the allegations you—"

"OK, forget about me for now. We have to stop them from hanging Palma tomorrow."

"Hanging, drawing and quartering, *and* stepping on his brains is the actual sentence."

"Yeah, I want to stop it all."

"Let me explain to you that under the present laws in Laranja East there are only two ways to save a man from the gallows." He held up his hand and noticed one of his fingernails was split and paused to suck at it. "One, a Royal Pardon from the king. Two, a Will of God Reprieve from the Territorial Pope."

"The pope sounds like our best bet. How soon can we see him?"

"We can't. He's in St. Charlie's," replied the lawyer. "Therefore, in actuality, our only hope is the king."

"Huh," said Summer, mostly to himself.

"I think I had best explain, Mr. Summer, that the earliest possible appointment I can probably get with the Screening Committee which passes on who shall see the king would be next month sometime. This leads me to conclude—"

"Princess Joline will have to do it," decided Summer.

"The princess cannot legally—"

"She can persuade her father; she'll have to."

"She's nearly as difficult to see as—"

"I'll take care of contacting her." The blond princess was waiting for him back at the den of thieves. "Thank you for your time and trouble. Dr. Roarer will see you safely out of Suicide Slum."

The lawyer eyed the foot specialist. "I'd rather risk it on my own," he said.

Princess Joline was sitting, in a sort of discarded rag-doll position, in the wood and leather chair in the corner of Summer's room. The TV-ball floated, blank and silent, near her lovely head. Her eyes were moist, red rimmed. "Actually it's all for the best," she said. "Although . . ."

Summer continued across the room. "Listen, Joline, there's only one way to get Palma free."

"Though I am in an awkward position as to—"

"The lawyers can't do a damn thing, or won't. So you've got to help."

"To hear it like this on television." The princess began sniffing, putting one slender finger under her nose.

"So I want you to go home," said Summer, stopping

before her. "Go to the palace, talk to your father, convince him he's going to be in a hell of a lot of trouble all over the universe if he allows Palma to be executed. If we had more time I could get Coult to put pressure on various—"

"Or don't know whether to be heartbroken or glad really."

"You tell your father that Coult will fix it so Laranja East never gets another drop of aid from Barnum and he'll get a bad press on every planet in the Barnum System. Then you tell him he's got to issue a Royal Pardon for Palma, and the girl."

The girl took hold of one of his hands in both of hers. "You don't understand what I've been telling you?"

"I guess I wasn't paying enough attention. What?"

"My father's found out about my part in the escape of you and Dr. Ferrier and the rest," Joline said. "He was just on television talking about it. He even threw my portrait, the one done by Van Horn, into the fireplace."

"OK, he's angry, but you still can—"

"It's gone beyond anger, Jack," she said. "He's publicly disowned me."

CHAPTER 22

———◆———

"Let's take it from the place where you mount the scaffold, Mr. Palma."

Palma sat down on the edge of the gallows platform, dangling his legs. Squinting at the glaring afternoon sun, he wiped perspiration from his bald head. "I didn't realize getting executed was such a chore."

"This isn't your everyday hanging, cookie," said the bouncing young man in the four-piece bottle-green worksuit. "This is a big one, a real bellringer of a public hanging." He was pacing the flagstone courtyard at the foot of the gibbet, nudging the assorted television and motion-picture cameramen into new positions, whispering instructions to others, of the score of technicians loitering there. "We've got, cookie, two of the most notorious highway robbers on the planet getting stretched at once. It's going to be a beaut."

Palma sighed out his breath. "Hutchison, you're obviously a well-informed lad," he said down at the bouncy producer-director of his execution. "Surely you've heard of me, Palma the photographer. I even won a Pulitzer Prize once, over in the Earth System of Planets. I'm no highwayman."

Hutchison was conferring with a technician. "We're

140

going to have to do something about your head," he
called to Palma.

"The Robot Magistrate already told me about that."

"No, no, I mean while you're still alive. We're getting a glare."

"We might postpone the execution until an overcast
day," suggested Palma.

"Not on your tintype, cookie. You and the Scarlet
Angel take off at noon, come rain or come shine.
Freddie, do something about Mr. Palma's head."

Freddie, a small catman, bounded up the gallows
steps flourishing a makeup case. "Have you present-
able in a minute, cookie."

"You could call the Coult Publications rep in the
capital," Palma said to Hutchison. "He'll tell you I'm
universally renowned."

Hutchison had his head close to that of a very old
lizardman. "Boots thinks you're not properly defiant,
Mr. Palma," he said through cupped hands. "Can you
give us a little more defiance mounting the steps?"

"How about a few obscene gestures?"

"No, no, cookie. We've got our kid audience to
think about. A nice defiant shake of the fist might be
exactly what we want."

"Hey," said Palma, "I think my hanging from a rope
is going to scare those tykes more than a thrown finger. Why don't we change it to a fine and probation?"

A blue-haired black man had been telling Hutchison something. "Gurney here thinks you'd look better
cringing than defiant. Want to give us a few sample
cringes, Mr. Palma?"

"No. It's my execution and I'd rather do it defiant."

An anxious-looking young man popped out of one

of the TV trucks. "Let's get the rehearsal rolling again, if we may, Hutch," he said. "I've got to have my crew at the public horsewhippings by two."

"Can we step livelier, Mr. Palma?"

After a moment of watching the trucks and the distant iron gates of the stone-walled prison yard, Palma said, "Soon as Freddie's through with my head."

"All done, cookie." Freddie administered one final pat of powder before bounding down the steps.

"Very well, Mr. Palma, from the top if you please."

Palma stood up. "I'd feel more natural if the Scarlet Angel could join me for—"

"No, no, that's bad luck," Hutchison told him. "You shouldn't see her till the real execution."

"This isn't a wedding."

"Listen, cookie, I've produced more executions than you can imagine. It's better the participants don't get a look at each other until the—"

Bam Bam! Bam!

"Will you, for the love of goodness, stop that pounding."

Bam! Bam! Bam!

"We got to get this goddamn royal viewing-stand finished in time for the hanging, goddamn it!" The lizard carpenter on the half-completed stand shook his hammer at Hutchison.

"What royal viewing-stand?"

"This goddamn royal reviewing-stand, for the goddamn king to sit his goddamn ass on."

Hutchison scowled. "Nobody told me the king was going to attend."

"Well, he is."

Bam! Bam! Bam!

"Now I'll have to give him ten minutes of my execution for denying he's the Phantom of the Fog," said the producer-director. "I'm really getting weary of this sort of thing, King Waldo barging in on my executions and stealing the spotlight from—"

"Tell him about *noblesse oblige*," said Palma as he climbed, slowly, down the scaffold steps.

Bam! Bam! Bam!

Palma glanced around him. The farthest TV truck was only a hundred feet from the gates. It looked tough enough to smash the iron gates off their hinges. "I've been thinking," Palma said to Hutchison, "I might want to sign up with Criminal Exploitations after all. Are Bert and Howie around?"

"They're beyond help."

"Meaning what?"

"Both of them had complete nervous breakdowns and had to be rushed to St. Charlie's."

"A hospital?"

"A loony bin," said Hutchison. "But we can't chitchat all day. Let's run through your last walk once more, cookie."

Someone suddenly bumped into Palma from behind.

"Oops, sorry. Who is that?" The hangman had arrived, large, stripped to the waist, black hooded.

"We don't want any clumsy hangmen around here, Spingarn," warned Hutchison.

"I'm not Spingarn, I'm Lizorty." The hangman stumbled into Palma once again. "Spingarn is laid up with the vapors and a touch of brain fever."

"OK, OK. Climb up on the platform, Lizorty. Stand there with your arms folded, looking tough."

"Yes, I'll certainly try to convey ... oops, I'm afraid I've bumped into you yet another time, sir. Who did you say you were?"

"I'm Palma, the star of the festivities."

"Oh, you're one of the ones I'll be hanging tomorrow, do you mean?" asked the hangman. "This is really much more difficult than I was led to believe. For instance, I can barely see out of this darned hood."

"You've got it on backward."

"Is that it? I'm glad you told me. This is my first try at being a hangman."

"I'll help you straighten it." Palma moved around in back of the broad Lizorty. He took hold of the bottom of the hood with one hand, then grabbed the hangman's wrist and pulled his arm tight up behind his back.

"Hey, ow! That hurts."

"Walk," ordered Palma. "Straight ahead. We're going to borrow a truck."

"This is my first day as a hangman, I can't go skylarking around—"

"Walk!"

"Ow! Very well."

With the hangman serving as a shield, Palma headed toward the truck he'd eyed earlier. "Everybody stand back or I'll throttle Lizorty here."

"Oops ... tripped on something."

"A cable. Step over it, keep walking."

Hutchison said, "You're simply holding everybody up, Mr. Palma. You can't possibly escape."

Palma gripped the hangman's thick neck. "Try to stop me and it's curtains for your brand-new hangman."

The bouncy young man took a stungun out of his pocket. "Stop right there. Mr. Palma."

Still fifty feet from the truck he had in mind, Palma said, "I'm warning you. I'll strangle this guy."

"Go ahead," said Hutchison. "Then we can get a fresh hangman over and get back to rehearsing your hanging." He walked right up to Palma and pressed the nose of the gun to his neck.

"OK, you asked for it." He allowed a few seconds to pass, then let go of his hostage. "I guess I can't strangle him."

"I knew that, cookie." As the hangman stumbled away, Hutchison put his stungun away. "Whenever you're ready, Mr. Palma."

CHAPTER 23

———◆———

"Get your Palma balloons! Get your Palma balloons!" shouted the enormous catwoman as she rattled several inflated ones in the air. "A striking likeness to the devilish rogue!"

A one-armed old man bellowed, "Buy your copies of *The True and Shocking Memoirs of the Ruthless Scarlet Angel, Together with Details of Her Lustful Days with Palma, the Bald Assassin!* 'Couldn't put it down,' says Abel of the *Laranja Bulletin*. 'A joy to read!' says Sheldorf of the *Express*. Lurid, racy, unputdownable! Paperback rights sold for a six-figure amount."

"Palma on a horse! Palma on a horse!"

"Authentic reproduction of an oil painting of Scarlet Angel in a state of undress!"

"Palma and Angel spoon and fork set!"

Splat!

A ripe vegetable, something pale blue he couldn't identify, hit Palma over the left eye. As he was wiping it off a tomato hit him in the chest. "Now that I recognize," he said.

He was riding along, alone, in an open horse-drawn cart. In the cart ahead rode the Scarlet Angel. There were at least two thousand people packed into the prison courtyard, not including the television, radio, and film crews. The noon sun blazed a smutty orange.

"Aid the sightless, sir." A yellow-bearded blind man in purple-tinted glasses had made his way to the side of the slow-rolling gallows wagon.

"How about you aid me?" asked Palma. "All you have to do is—"

"Stall them," the blind man said.

The bald photographer blinked. "Jack?"

The blind man was gone, back into the pushing, shouting crowd.

Palma poked the tip of his tongue into his cheek. The Scarlet Angel glanced back at him at that instant. He smiled at her.

She smiled back, but sadly.

The viewing-stand was perched on gold-painted posts several feet above the ground, trimmed with considerable blue and gold bunting. King Waldo II and a dozen government and prison officials were already seated there, protected from the bright sun by a blue and gold awning.

The king sat with his crown in his lap. "I think, Warden Heartloft, we ought to schedule all future public executions late in the day."

The fluffy-furred catman leaned toward the monarch. "Blame it on the media, your highness. They inform me the light's better at midday."

King Waldo wiped his hand across his stubbly cheek. "I know I personally enjoy an execution in the cool of the day. I will have to discuss this with Buzzkirk, my Minister of Public Communications."

Warden Heartloft coughed. "I do believe Buzzkirk

was hanged for high treason last month, your majesty."

"Yes, you're right, so he was, Heartloft. Well, I'll find out who the new man is and give him my views." He, sighing, replaced his crown on his head. "You should be thankful you don't have to wear a crown on a scorcher like today."

The warden chuckled. "The perils of kingship, eh?"

The carts had reached the foot of the scaffold. Two uniformed catmen lifted the Scarlet Angel out and set her on the lowest step.

"Up you go, sweet." One of them patted her on the backside.

"Hey, you overfamiliar bastard!" Palma leaped over the side of his cart and hurled himself at the offending guard.

The catman groped for his shockstick.

Palma got an elbow into his stomach before he reached the weapon. "Let's maintain a little dignity for this execution," he said.

The guard fell over on the flagstones, and Palma stepped on his face.

The crowd screamed, hooted, laughed.

"Bloody murder!"

"Public outrage!"

"Slit the skinhead's gullet!"

"Step on his knackers, Baldy!"

"Bravo!"

The other guard cracked Palma across the back of his neck with his shockstick, causing him to go stumbling toward the steps.

"Palma." The Scarlet Angel caught him and kept him from falling. "'Tis much too late to fight."

It was some seconds before the power of speech returned. "I'm stalling."

"Whatever for?"

"To save our lives, I hope."

The fallen guard had arisen. "Ah, just you wait, me lad," he snarled. "When it comes time to slice you open I'll do a special dance on your innards."

"May you slip and bust your hairy ass." Palma took hold of the red-haired girl's arm and escorted her, wobbling a bit, up to the gallows.

The hangman bowed to the Scarlet Angel. "Good morning, miss. I'm Lizorty, your hangman. I'll attempt to makes things as comfortable as possible for you." He shook his head at Palma, turning his back on him.

"Snubbed by my own hangman. I thought you were above pettiness, Lizorty."

"You nearly ruined my career, nipped it in the bud as it were," said the bulky hangman. "I got a perishing talking-to after your antics yesterday."

Clatter! Clatter! Bump!

"In the name of the lord, go easy, you buffoons!"

The guards at the foot of the stairs were attempting to help a plump birdman in clerical garb to ascend. He was strapped to a wheelchair.

"Suppose I carry you, Bishop, and my mate hefts the chair," suggested the one Palma had stepped on.

"Imbeciles! Clowns! The chair is attached to me by several life-giving tubes and wires. Would you have the Archbishop of Laranja East perish here in the shadow of the gibbet?"

"Not any shadows at high noon, your grace."

"I was speaking allegorically, you dolt. Hurry,

hurry now. I have to administer the last rites to this pair of vipers."

"We'll surely try, your grace."

"Who's that?" The hangman stuck a thumb under the lip of his black hood. "I still can't see too well out of this damn thing."

"Appears to be a birdman dressed up like a bishop," said Palma, grinning.

"Oh, that must be Archbishop O'Malley J. O'Malley. A fine god-fearing man, though a bit crusty since his speedboat accident. He'll do you a splendid last rites," said Lizorty. "Be careful, though, should you decide to repent at the last moment and kiss his ring. There's a sharp edge on it and you're likely to slice your—"

"There, there, that's more like it." With considerable further clatter and bumping the archbishop was placed on the platform between the Scarlet Angel and Palma. "You may kiss my ring if you like, you churls," he said, holding out a feathery hand to the guards.

"Meaning no offense, your grace, but—"

"Never mind, then. Clear the deck and let's get rolling." He rubbed his hands together, his golden ring flashing in the sunlight. "Oh, Lord, I ask you to grant—"

"Hsst. Hsst."

The Archbishop's head darted from left to right several times. "What's that?"

It was Hutchison, the producer-director, peering up over the back of the platform. "Hold that ladder steady, cookie," he told someone down below. "Can you hold off on your blessing for about five minutes?"

"Lad, I've a wake and two heresy trials to attend before sundown. I can't ..."

"Turns out there's some girl from the King Waldo Civic Clubs who's got a bouquet to present to him. See her down there by the viewing-stand?"

The Archbishop leaned over and gave his miter a poke. "Ah, yes, a comely lass."

A dark-haired girl, wearing black-tinted glasses and a pure white dressing, was climbing the steps toward the king. A huge bunch of yellow flowers was clutched in her hands.

Close to the birdman Palma said, "Your grace, I'm struck by the uncanny resemblance between you and certain members of the Starbuck clan. Would you be related?"

"Don't blow my disguise yet," whispered Mulligan Starbuck. "Watch this next bit of business. Should it not work, we'll have a tough time indeed."

As the girl presented the flowers to the smiling King Waldo a cloud of greenish mist suddenly sprayed out of the bouquet and into his face.

Mulligan wheeled to the edge of the platform and grabbed a public-address mike. "Citizens of Laranja East, you are about to learn the real identity of the Phantom of the Fog," he said. "Yes, the Phantom is, despite all his protests to the contrary, your own King Waldo."

"What?"

"Impossible!"

"Told you so!"

"What'd he say?"

The spray was having its effect on the king. He tossed away his crown, made growling noises, hunched down. He snatched up the warden's slouch hat and pulled it down tight on his head. Ripping a large piece of bunting down, he flung it over his shoulders to make a cape. "Old ladies," he roared. "Boy, do I hate 'em! Old ladies, what do they know? Tell you when to brush your teeth, when to go to bed. Ugh, I hate 'em!" His hands formed clutching claws and, with a growl, he ran down the steps, knocked aside the bouquet girl, and threw himself at the crowd. "There's one! There's an old biddy. Ugh! Let me get my mitts on her! Let me strangle her!"

The girl stood up and pulled off the black wig she was wearing. She climbed to the viewing-stand to take hold of a microphone. "My people, I am Princess Joline," she announced.

"Oh!"

"Ah!"

"Thought so!"

"Pretty, ain't she?"

"I am sorry, sorrier than any of you, that I had to do what I did. There was, however, no other way. The people who stand on yonder gallows are innocent. In order to save them I was forced to reveal my father's awful secret."

"Grr! Grr! Let me at that old dame!" Ten or more citizens were sitting on or holding parts of the crazed monarch.

"I say to you now," said Joline, "that the reign of injustice is over. I am the rightful heiress to the throne, as you well know. I, therefore, proclaim myself queen of this territory. Should any man oppose me, let him speak out." She turned to the dozen on the stand.

They shifted in their chairs, coughed, but said nothing.

"Long live the queen!" shouted a lone voice in the crowd.

"That's Jack Summer," said Palma.

"Long live the queen!"

"Long live the queen!"

Soon the entire throng was chanting it.

The hangman took off his hood. "Well, there's another botch."

Palma led the Scarlet Angel to the edge of the scaffold. They both sat down, feet swinging. "We're innocent," he told her.

"I don't feel so very innocent."

"You can't argue with the queen."

"No, I suppose not." She put her arms around him.

CHAPTER 24

———◆———

Palma came into their spaceliner cabin with bright flecks of confetti dotting his head. "You're missing a considerable frolic," he said, unwinding a yellow streamer from around his ear.

Summer was sitting at a wheeled talkwriter, the mike swinging in his hand. "I want to finish up this Phantom piece."

"Captain's birthday party it is." The photographer ambled to a worktable which had several sheets of photographic proofs spread out on it. "You should have seen the first mate dancing on the bar."

"Gifted, is he?"

"A lady, the first mate is a young lady. You have never witnessed such yonkers, Jack. Shaped exactly like ... you know, those melons you always get for breakfast on Murdstone."

"I usually have juice and cereal."

Palma rested both hands on the table edge, studying the pictures he'd taken on Peregrine. "You're in one of your glum moods again," he observed. "After every assignment you become very dour. I'm going to miss those knockers...." He held up some tiny contact shots of the Scarlet Angel. "You know, Queen Joline doesn't have a bad set of hangers herself. These pix of the coronation bring that out. Not very many coronations I've covered here and there across this old universe of ours have involved a girl with such exemplary equipment. Although once on—"

"Why don't you go back up and dance on the bar?"

Palma said, "I can't actually, Jack." He started brushing the bits of colored paper off himself. "The captain suggested I withdraw from the celebration. There's some nitwit space-naval regulation about fondling a ship's officer. I didn't think it applied to girl first mates, but he insisted and since it's his birthday and since our cabin is a shade more comfortable than the brig . . ."

Summer hung up the mike, clicked off the talkwriter, and pushed it aside. "OK, tell me about the first mate's bosom."

Tapping the camera hanging around his neck, Palma said, "Show you the pictures later." He looked again at the sheets of pictures. "This puts you one up on me. I've never slept with a real queen."

"She was only a princess at the time."

"Oh, so? You mean after she took the throne you never . . . you spent a lot of time with her at the palace."

"Joline wanted me to stay in Laranja East."

"Hey, you mean as king?"

"Nope, as her speech writer," replied Summer. "She feels a monarch should be clear and incisive."

"I suppose it's indicative of the differences in our character that you fall in with a princess and I with a highwayperson."

"The Scarlet Angel's reformed, remember? She's Joline's Minister of Justice now."

"Yeah, but she's best suited to outdoor work." Palma picked up another sheet of photos. "Here's Dr. Ferrier being sworn in as the new Secretary of Peace. Good thing he had an extra supply of his Special Blend Number Three for Joline to squirt on her papa."

"He didn't. The stuff we used at your execution was a new batch made up with ingredients scrounged up in Suicide Slum."

Palma was considering another string of photos. "Mulligan Starbuck, or whatever his name is, looks pretty good in this diplomatic outfit," he said. "I got some nice stuff of his negotiating the cease-fire between East and West. Ah, and here's St. Charlie's with all the inmates being let free. Who's this red-bearded lad with the two black eyes?"

"Dr. Brownlove," said Summer from where he sat. "He's the guy who supervised my torture. I had a chance to see him when St. Charlie's was liberated."

"This angora catman looks a little odd. Didn't notice him at the time."

Summer went over to look. "That's a real lunatic. They let him out with the rest."

Palma shuffled the proof sheets, got them into an even pile, and dropped it to the table. "Things should go well in Laranja East from now on."

"Maybe," said Summer. "Is that party still going on up there?"

"Sure, why?"

"Think I'll go wish the captain a happy birthday." He crossed to the cabin door.

"OK," said Palma. "If you're not back in a couple of hours I'll check the brig."

DAW BOOKS

Presenting JOHN NORMAN in DAW editions . . .

☐ **TRIBESMEN OF GOR.** The tenth novel of Tarl Cabot takes him face to face with the Others' most dangerous plot— in the vast Tahari desert with its warring tribes, its bandit queen, and its treachery.   (#UW1223—$1.50)

☐ **HUNTERS OF GOR.** The saga of Tarl Cabot on Earth's orbital counterpart reaches a climax as Tarl seeks his lost Talena among the outlaws and panther women of the wilderness.   (#UW1102—$1.50)

☐ **MARAUDERS OF GOR.** The ninth novel of Tarl Cabot's adventures takes him to the northland of transplanted Vikings and into direct confrontation with the enemies of two worlds.   (#UW1160—$1.50)

☐ **TIME SLAVE.** The creator of Gor brings back the days of the caveman in a vivid new novel of time travel and human destiny.   (#UW1204—$1.50)

☐ **IMAGINATIVE SEX.** A study of the sexuality of male and female which leads to a new revelation of sensual libera-tion. Fifty-three imaginative situations are outlined, some of which are science-fictional in nature.
                    (#UJ1146—$1.95)

DAW BOOKS are represented by the publishers of Signet and Mentor Books, THE NEW AMERICAN LIBRARY, INC.

DAW=sf BOOKS

Lin Carter's bestselling series!

☐ **UNDER THE GREEN STAR.** A marvel adventure in the grand tradition of Burroughs and Merritt. Book I.
(#UY1185—$1.25)

☐ **WHEN THE GREEN STAR CALLS.** Beyond Mars shines the beacon of exotic adventure. Book II. (#UY1267—$1.25)

☐ **BY THE LIGHT OF THE GREEN STAR.** Lost amid the giant trees, nothing daunted his search for his princess and her crown. Book III. (#UY1268—$1.25)

☐ **AS THE GREEN STAR RISES.** Adrift on the uncharted sea of a nameless world, hope still burned bright. Book IV.
(#UY1156—$1.25)

☐ **IN THE GREEN STAR'S GLOW.** The grand climax of an adventure amid monsters and marvels of a far-off world. Book V. (#UY1216—$1.25)

DAW BOOKS are represented by the publishers of Signet and Mentor Books, THE NEW AMERICAN LIBRARY, INC.

THE NEW AMERICAN LIBRARY, INC.,
P.O. Box 999, Bergenfield, New Jersey 07621

Please send me the DAW BOOKS I have checked above. I am enclosing $_____(check or money order—no currency or C.O.D.'s). Please include the list price plus 35¢ a copy to cover mailing costs.

Name_____

Address_____

City_____State_____Zip Code_____
Please allow at least 3 weeks for delivery

ANDRE NORTON
in DAW BOOKS editions

- [ ] **PERILOUS DREAMS.** Tamisen could dream true—and the worlds she entered were actual realms of peril! The 1976 Norton-of-the-year! (#UY1237—$1.25)

- [ ] **MERLIN'S MIRROR.** A brand-new novel, written for DAW, of science-lore versus Arthurian legendry. (#UY1175—$1.25)

- [ ] **SPELL OF THE WITCH WORLD.** A DAW exclusive, continuing the famous Witch World stories, and not available elsewhere. (#UY1179—$1.25)

- [ ] **THE CRYSTAL GRYPHON.** The latest in the beloved Witch World novels, it is an outstanding other-world adventure. (#UY1187—$1.25)

- [ ] **HERE ABIDE MONSTERS.** Trapped in a parallel world, just off Earth's own map and right out of legend. (#UY1134—$1.25)

- [ ] **GARAN THE ETERNAL.** An epic adventure in lost worlds and unmeasured time—never before in paperbacks. (#UY1186—$1.25)

- [ ] **THE BOOK OF ANDRE NORTON.** Novelettes, short stories, articles, and a bibliography make this a treat for Norton's millions of readers. (#UY1198—$1.25)

DAW BOOKS are represented by the publishers of Signet and Mentor Books, THE NEW AMERICAN LIBRARY, INC.

THE NEW AMERICAN LIBRARY, INC.,
P.O. Box 999, Bergenfield, New Jersey 07621

Please send me the DAW BOOKS I have checked above. I am enclosing
$_____(check or money order—no currency or C.O.D.'s).
Please include the list price plus 35¢ a copy to cover mailing costs.

Name_____

Address_____

City_____State_____Zip Code_____
Please allow at least 3 weeks for delivery

DAW sf BOOKS